WARFARE
CIVIL WAR

also by Alex Garland from Faber

28 DAYS LATER
THE COMA
SUNSHINE
NEVER LET ME GO (SCREENPLAY)
DREDD
DEVS
ANNIHILATION

WARFARE

screenplay by
RAY MENDOZA &
ALEX GARLAND

CIVIL WAR

screenplay by
ALEX GARLAND

faber

First published in 2025
by Faber & Faber Limited
The Bindery, 51 Hatton Garden
London ECIN 8HN

First published in the USA in 2025

Typeset by Faber & Faber Limited
Printed and bound in Canada

Warfare screenplay © 2025 Real Time Situation LLC. All Rights Reserved
Civil War screenplay © 2023 Miller Avenue Rights LLC. All Rights Reserved

The rights of Alex Garland and Ray Mendoza to be identified as authors of this work have been asserted in accordance with Section 77 of the Copyright, Designs and Patents Act 1988

A CIP record for this book is available from the British Library

ISBN 978–0–571–39370–1

Our authorised representative in the EU for product safety is
Easy Access System Europe, Mustamäe tee 50, 10621 Tallinn, Estonia
gpsr.requests@easproject.com

2 4 6 8 10 9 7 5 3

Contents

Introduction vii

WARFARE

The Screenplay 1

CIVIL WAR

The Screenplay 103

Warfare & Civil War

An interview with Ray Mendoza by Walter Donohue

Walter Donohue

Several months ago Alex Garland told me that he was writing a screenplay based on an incident that occurred in Iraq when a group of Navy SEALs became trapped in a house, surrounded by insurgents. In the ensuing violence, two lost their lives and three were seriously wounded.

In order to capture the visceral reality of the conflict, Alex felt that the screenplay needed to be pared down, an approach that was very different from the one he took when writing *Civil War*. This was the point at which I had the idea of publishing a book that juxtaposed the screenplays of *Warfare* and *Civil War* to highlight just how different *Warfare* is.

Alex co-wrote the script and co-directed the film with Ray Mendoza, who was there in that house.

Give me some insight into the process of writing the script with Alex.

Ray Mendoza

It was a story I had wanted to tell for a really long time. But the response I got to what I wrote was 'Who's the hero, what's the hero's journey, what's his backstory, what's the premise, what's the arc?' It broke all those rules.

Alex and I wanted to tell the story in a different way. So, we took a very forensic approach – it was a re-creation, but done as if we were doing a documentary, interviewing the people who were there, diving deeper into the situation. We gathered together the guys who were under attack in that house and asked questions, such as 'What were you feeling?'

Of course, they were all young – 'I'm not scared, I'm strong, I don't have feelings about what was happening.' A survival mechanism kicks in in order to be functional in a war environment. At the time, we didn't have the verbiage to convey what we felt that day.

vii

Of course, I have my memories of what happened, and I knew that, in preparing the actors, I needed to express how I was afraid, how I was supposed to perform. Even though I was trained for this kind of conflict, to this day I'm still ashamed of actions I should have done quicker, or better – we're our own worst critics.

But Alex and I didn't want the film to be just from my perspective. That would only produce big holes in the story. So, each time we interviewed someone, that section of the film became more fleshed out. There was the confusion, you're trying to figure out what's happening; what action should you take, why did you make the decisions that you did, and how do you feel about that now?

Back in the day of silent films, we would sense what a character was feeling through the expression on his face – that's kind of what we were trying to achieve in *Warfare*. You'll see a lot of looks between the guys – we didn't want to fall into the trap of explanatory dialogue, like 'Oh, my girlfriend just left me.' So we tried to express the relationship between characters, convey those kind of emotional states through looks and reactions.

What we are trying to do is to draw the audience into the world of the film and share with them what the characters are thinking and feeling: what it feels like to be scared, what it feels like to be confused, what it feels like to struggle to overcome the violence that you're encountering, and how far willpower can take you.

Once that first grenade goes off, it's just like – they'd often say to me, 'I can't believe it went so fast . . . I can breathe now.'

You can choose to forget as time passes, your mind tends to normalise these experiences. You forget but, as we worked through things, they started coming back, 'Oh shit, I'd forgotten about that.' Like the blood. Arterial blood is different from ordinary blood – it has a metallic odour. Just thinking about it makes me gag.

Memories are tricky things. As I was talking with the guys about their memories, my own memories started to surface. When the guys were remembering, they'd say something that caused me to remember, then I'd say something that caused them to remember. There's certain parts – like when I was with my friend Elliott – where I remembered what it smelled like, what it sounded like, or the lack of sound. When you put so much of your emotion into it – I was frozen – it felt like an eternity, but I'm sure it was only thirty seconds, which is still, in a gunfight, a long time.

I went into a lot of detail explaining it to Alex; then we spent a long time re-creating it.

Me and my friends, we just didn't want to deal with it – kept pushing it down. But the monster will catch up with you eventually. You want to explain it, you want to share it with your wife, brother, sister, but you just don't have the vocabulary, or you're not ready to share it. I'd never really talked about it to anyone before Alex and, though I was ready, it was hard – the rush of emotions that it caused!

The film isn't just my perspective, it's of every one of us who was there – and watching the finished film has helped me accept what we went through.

Alex is an angel – he helped me a lot. He's a great collaborator, open-minded. Working together was something special – how we approached it, how we executed it; the cast were completely on board. It was the perfect recipe and I'm glad I did it with him.

WARFARE

Written by Ray Mendoza and Alex Garland

SHOOTING SCRIPT 2 May 13th

HOLD ON THE BLACK SCREEN.

A beat.

Then, in white lettering –

CAPTION:

> November 19th, 2006. Ramadi, Iraq.
>
> A Navy SEAL platoon takes sniper positions in support of a US Marines Operation.

The CAPTIONS disappear.

New CAPTION:

> This film uses only their memories.

The CAPTION disappears.

Then **CUT TO** –

1   <u>**EXT. RAMADI/STREET – NIGHT**</u>   1

– a group of twenty-two soldiers.

They are walking down a street in the Iraqi city of RAMADI, Al Anbar Province, 75 miles west of Baghdad.

The soldiers are a mixture of –

– NAVY SEALS, TEAM 5: an elite Special Operations unit within the US Navy. NAVY SEALS are most famous with the public for the killing of Osama bin Laden, but much of their work is covert and unreported.

– MARINES: another fighting arm of the US Navy. Less elite than the SEALS, but highly trained, with a long history of front-line combat.

– IRAQI SCOUTS: local soldiers, placed with US military as part of a programme to train the Iraqi military in specialist US fighting tactics. They also act as interpreters.

The soldiers move in single file.

NOTE: ELLIOTT is on point.

3.

They are alert.

Tense, scanning, weapons up.

No one talks.

They are entering an enemy stronghold - this section of RAMADI has been so dangerous to enter that the US military fully withdrew from area three months ago.

This is the first time since the withdrawal that any US military have returned.

We view this NIGHT SEQUENCE as the soldiers do: through NIGHT VISION GOGGLES.

The NVGs are pulled down from the helmets, over their eyes.

It makes the soldiers anonymous to us. Almost indistinguishable from one another.

It shows the world in shades of GREEN, BLACK, and WHITE.

Through the NVG vision, we can see little of the city.

A dusty road, litter-strewn.

Lined with concrete houses, mostly set back, behind high walls.

2   **EXT. RAMADI/JUNCTION - NIGHT**   2

The SOLDIERS reach a junction.

They split into groups.

OP-1, OP-2, and OP-3.

We stay with OP-1.

Ten men.

3   **EXT. RAMADI/STREET - NIGHT**   3

OP-1 approaches one of the houses on the street.

It is a two-storey concrete building, set back from the road, behind a six-foot wall and a metal GATE.

Between the gate and the building, there is a small DRIVEWAY, with a scrubby garden on one side.

At the end of the driveway, there is a second wall, with a strip of patterned air bricks to let a breeze through.

It creates a small covered COURTYARD around the front entrance.

On the second floor of the house, there is a BALCONY.

OP-1 stack up by the front wall.

Two of the soldiers are boosted over.

Moments later, they quietly open the metal gate.

As a group, OP-1 moves silently up the driveway.

Four of the soldiers keep their focus ahead - at the house.

The others cover all surrounding angles: rooftops, overlooking windows, their rear.

The four leading soldiers stack up by front door.

A beat.

A go-sign from the lead soldier - lifting the barrel of his gun, then dipping it.

Then -

- the front door is quietly opened.

The four-man entry team move inside the building.

4   **INT. HOUSE/KITCHEN - NIGHT**   4

Silence, caution, and stealth are still maintained.

The four-man entry team enter the room - a KITCHEN.

They sweep with their weapons.

Seconds later they are moving to the doorway that leads deeper into the house.

As this next doorway is breached -

- the rest of OP-1 are flooding into the kitchen.

5   **INT. HOUSE/HALL - NIGHT**   5

We follow the entry team into the next space.

A HALL, with two rooms to the left, and stairs leading up to the right.

6   **INT. HOUSE/STAIRS - NIGHT**   6

Two of the soldiers move up the stairs.

We stay with them.

We hear the sound of an IRAQI MAN suddenly calling out in alarm.

5.

7 **INT. HOUSE/UPSTAIRS MAIN ROOM - NIGHT** 7

The top of the stairs opens into a room -

- where we glimpse an IRAQI family.

Jolted awake from sleep.

Waking into a nightmare.

A MAN and a WOMAN - emerging from their bedrooms.

They are actually a brother and sister.

The woman is widowed.

Behind her are her daughters - two young GIRLS, through the doorway of another room, aged seven and nine.

The MAN starts pleading.

The WOMAN starts screaming.

Then the two young GIRLS start screaming and crying.

We see their terrified faces in GREEN, BLACK, and WHITE.

ABRUPTLY -

CUT TO -

8 **EXT. RAMADI - DAY** 8

- morning over RAMADI.

An aerial view.

Now we can see the city.

A mass of concrete buildings, clustered along the banks of the Euphrates River.

9 **EXT. HOUSE - DAY** 9

We revisit the exterior of the two-storey concrete house that the soldiers have occupied.

Now in daylight.

The WALLS.

The GATE.

CUT TO -

10 **EXT. HOUSE/DRIVEWAY - DAY**   10

The DRIVEWAY.

Wide enough for one vehicle.

Long enough for two vehicles.

CUT TO -

11 **EXT. HOUSE/COURTYARD - DAY**   11

- the covered COURTYARD at the end of the driveway.

The high wall with air bricks.

The FRONT ENTRANCE of the house.

CUT TO -

12 **EXT. HOUSE/BALCONY - DAY**   12

- the BALCONY, wrapped around the front and side of the
house.

On the balcony are four CLAYMORES.

Curved cases, containing directional explosive charges, set
out along the balcony in a daisy chain.

There is also a ROVER III COMMS RECIEVER.

It looks like a white hockey puck sat on three stubby legs,
and relays images from air support down to OP-1.

A cable runs from the ROVER III, back into the house, through
a metal door, slightly ajar.

The houses either side are close enough that one could almost
step from the roof of one house to the next.

CUT TO -

13 **INT. HOUSE/DOWNSTAIRS BEDROOM - DAY**   13

- the ground-floor bedroom, just off the main living area.

The IRAQI FAMILY are sitting together on the bed.

Keeping guard over the family is an IRAQI SCOUT - SIDAR.

SIDAR is 31.

He holds an Israeli-made AK-47 assault rifle.

SIDAR is smoking.

7.

The MAN sits on the edge of the bed, looking at the ground.

The two young girls are lying in middle of the bed, calmer than we last saw them.

They are huddled up to their MOTHER, who is watching SIDAR.

SIDAR is ignoring them all.

Staring into space, concentrating on his cigarette.

He looks tense, but bored.

CUT TO -

14   **INT. HOUSE/HALL - DAY**   14

- an empty HALL, just outside the downstairs bedroom.

A flight of stairs leads up to the second floor.

At the end of the hall is the KITCHEN.

CUT TO -

15   **INT. HOUSE/KITCHEN - DAY**   15

- the kitchen.

The first room in the house that OP-1 entered.

In daylight, we can see that it contains a concrete shelf, built out of the wall.

On the shelf is a small propane stove, some pots and pans, and a small stack of mismatched plates.

The FRONT ENTRANCE, leading to the outside courtyard, is being covered by two soldiers.

The first is TOMMY.

TOMMY is 21. He's white.

A NAVY SEAL.

This is TOMMY'S first platoon. As someone young, and new to front-line operations, he is sometimes called 'Meat' - as in, fresh meat.

He's stocky. He makes up for his short stature by being good at stuff. He can use a fifty-calibre machine gun with precision. Unlike some SEALS, he's not showy. His dad and brother were SEALS before him.

TOMMY is a GUNNER. He is armed with a MK 48 MACHINE GUN.

Behind TOMMY is a second IRAQI SCOUT - FARID.

FARID is 30.

Like SIDAR, he carries an Israeli AK-47.

Like SIDAR, FARID is smoking.

None of them are talking.

16   **INT. HOUSE/MAIN BEDROOM - DAY**   16

- the parents' main bedroom.

Upstairs, off the MAIN ROOM.

The double bed has a metal frame.

The floor has rugs. Family photos hang on the walls.

There are also specific and slightly random pieces of decoration.

Three identical CERAMIC DOLPHINS on the window shelf.

A FELIX THE CAT CLOCK on the side table.

In this room, standing by the window, is SAM.

He's 28 years old.

White. Californian. A NAVY SEAL. Shaved head.

His position is Leading Petty Officer (LPO), technically second-in-command in OP-1.

SAM has a reputation for having a wild side. He starts pointless bar fights back home in the US, knowing that he has the backup of his pit bull Navy SEAL comrades.

He is holding his M4 assault rifle.

Propped against the wall is another weapon.

An M79 GRENADE LAUNCHER.

It's a Vietnam War-era weapon. Only the Navy SEALS continue to use it, because it's light, and small, and can be easily passed around.

Outside the window, there is a view over Ramadi rooftops.

The window has no glass. Just metal rebars for security, set into the concrete.

From outside, the sounds of the city drift in.

Car engines, prayer broadcasts from the nearest minaret, passing fragments of Arabic conversation.

SAM looks bored.

But also jittery.

CUT TO -

17   **INT. HOUSE/SNIPER ROOM - DAY**   17

- the room from which the two DAUGHTERS emerged, last night.

PEACH-COLOURED CURTAINS are drawn closed over a window.

Apart from those curtains, the room has been completely rearranged and repurposed by the soldiers.

Furniture has been pushed to the side.

A table has been brought in from the main room, and is draped in mats and rugs.

And a hole has been smashed in the exterior wall with a SLEDGEHAMMER - which is now propped in the dust and rubble on the floor of the room.

The hole is about twelve inches in diameter. Through them, there is a restricted view across the streets in this area of RAMADI.

A piece of netting/mesh is stretched over it.

It allows the sniper to see out, but makes it harder for people on the outside to see in.

And aiming through the hole, lying on the tables, kept comfortable by the mats and rugs -

- there is a SNIPER.

He is ELLIOTT.

ELLIOTT is 25.

He's white. From rural Illinois. A big man - built like a weightlifter, rather than a bodybuilder.

10.

ELLIOTT is the LEAD SNIPER of the platoon, and also the
MEDIC.

ELLIOTT is focused on the scope of his SR-25 rifle.

Sitting with his back against the wall, there is another
sniper. FRANK.

FRANK is 25.

White. He's an intelligent and highly effective soldier.
OCD with his gear - everything is clean and properly
positioned. He has a reputation as a 'fire and forget'
soldier, because if you task him with something, it will get
done.

CUT TO -

18   <u>**INT. HOUSE/UPSTAIRS KITCHEN-STORAGE - DAY**</u>   18

- an upstairs kitchen area, off the main room.

The room's a sink, some cupboards, and several bags of US AID
RICE.

Sat inside are two US Marines.

They are SGT 'LAERRUS' and LT MACDONALD.

LIEUTENANT MACDONALD is 27.

White. Short, skinny, moustache. He is a helicopter pilot,
but he has put himself on this mission to put in time on the
ground, and develop different experience. It's a route to
promotion up the ranks.

SERGEANT 'LAERRUS' is 24.

Black. Stocky, like TOMMY. East Coast.

LT MACDONALD and SGT LAERRUS are armed with standard-issue M4
assault rifles.

Both Marines are with OP-1 in an 'enabler' capacity, as part
of ANGLICO - there to support the Navy SEALS.

LT MACDONALD has a tough-case laptop computer - to which the
cable from the ROVER III COMMS RECIEVER runs.

On the laptop screen, there is a black-and-white LIVE FEED
from air support, showing their position and the surrounding
area.

LT MACDONALD is watching the screen closely, flicking between different feeds and magnifications.

CUT TO -

19   **INT. HOUSE/UPSTAIRS MAIN ROOM - DAY**   19

- the main room.

The hub room.

From here, stairs lead down to the first floor.

One doorway gives a view to where the SNIPERS lie.

A second doorway gives a view to the MAIN BEDROOM, where SAM stands by the window.

And a METAL DOOR leads out to the BALCONY.

This door can't close properly. Through the gap, one can see a sliver of DAYLIGHT.

Sat in this room, on rolled-up rugs and mats, near the door to the main bedroom, are the last two soldiers in OP-1.

The first is ERIK.

27 years old. White. Tall.

ERIK is the OIC - Officer-in-Charge. Leader of this platoon. Leader of OP-1.

To his men, he is viewed as a great officer - an enlisted man's officer. Not stuck-up or arrogant, as some officers can be. Inspiring, and relying intelligently on his team.

His rifle is an M4 with suppressor.

The second - and the last soldier in OP-1 - is RAY.

RAY is 24.

He has Mexican and Native American heritage.

He grew up in East LA, and had wanted to be a soldier as long as he could remember, as a way out of a home and neighbourhood he needed to leave behind. RAY liked the ocean, liked the water, so he joined the Navy at 17, and became a SEAL at 19.

12.

He is a specialist in JTAC - the man in the platoon who is in charge of radio communication and coordination with the RAMADI HQ, AIR SUPPORT, and ARTILLERY SUPPORT.

For this reason, he carries a radio pack - currently off his back, and sat beside him - and wears over-ear headphones.

His rifle is a ten-inch M4 with no suppressor.

Now, for the first time, someone speaks.

RAY - calling in to base on his radio.

He keeps his voice quiet.

NOTE: until the attack starts, ALL EXCHANGES ARE QUIETLY SPOKEN.

> RAY
> Manchu-6 X-Ray, this is Frogman-6 Romeo. Stand by for sitrep. Say when ready to copy. Over.

> MANCHU X-RAY
> (over radio)
> Frogman, send your traffic. Over.

> RAY
> (into radio)
> At zero-nine-seven, we observed people probing our position from the east, section Papa 1-0, building 1-7-4, east of route Boiler. At zero-nine-twelve we saw massing at building 1-7-5, north of route Spartan. Break.

Beat.

CONCURRENT -

> ERIK
> How's your signal?

> LT MACDONALD
> Now it's good, still intermittent.

> ERIK
> Okay. Cool.

BACK TO RAY -

                    RAY
          At zero-nine-sixteen, a blue Daewoo
          with MAMs north on route Lakers.
          How copy. Over.

                    MANCHU X-RAY
          Yeah - Frogman repeat everything
          after blue Daewoo. Over.

                    RAY
          Manchu, blue Daewoo with Military
          Age Males travelling north on
          Lakers.

                    MANCHU X-RAY
          Copy all. Do you have any more
          traffic for my station. Over.

                    RAY
          Negative, Manchu. Do you have any
          update for my station.

                    MANCHU X-RAY
          Roger that. Be advised, you have
          new friendly position. Baker
          Company has moved west of your
          position to your north, two
          kilometres. Over.

                    RAY
          Understand. Copy all. Frogman,
          out.

RAY glances at ERIK.

Holds up his map.

                    RAY (CONT'D)
          Sir. Baker Company were here.
          They're two kilometres, now here,
          in this position.

                    ERIK
          Copy that.

CUT TO -

20   <u>**INT. HOUSE/MAIN BEDROOM - DAY**</u>   20

- SAM.

Doing push-ups.

Once finished, he stands. Moves to the window.

Peering out.

He can see life in Ramadi.

A car driving.

Two women walking.

An older man and a young boy, walking in the opposite
direction.

In a window of a nearby building, he glimpses a figure. Just
for a moment.

Beats pass.

CUT TO -

21   **INT. HOUSE/UPSTAIRS KITCHEN-STORAGE - DAY**   21

- SGT LAERRUS and LT MACDONALD.

LT MACDONALD is staring at his laptop.

>   LT MACDONALD
>   North-east still clear.

>   SGT LAERRUS
>   Check that run of buildings to the
>   west again. You could step right
>   across those rooftops if you
>   wanted. Walk right to us.

LT MACDONALD cycles viewpoints.

Studies.

>   LT MACDONALD
>   Yessir. Got nothing.

CUT TO -

22   **INT. HOUSE/SNIPER ROOM - DAY**   22

- ELLIOTT.

Focused down his rifle scope.

Shifting view slightly.

15.

Then pausing.

Frowning slightly.

Not taking his eyes off his scope -

- he speaks to FRANK.

> ELLIOTT
> Got eyes on north-east corner of
> building four.

> FRANK
> Is the white Hilux still there?

> ELLIOTT
> It pulled out five minutes ago.
> Travelling north up Boiler. But
> I've got a male looking at our
> position. White shirt. Dark
> tracksuit pants. Sound familiar?
> Seen him at all?

> FRANK
> Negative. ID any weapons?

> ELLIOTT
> No weapons.

Beat.

> ELLIOTT (CONT'D)
> He's gone.

Beat.

> FRANK
> Is he going on the list?

ELLIOTT thinks a moment.

Then toggles his radio on.

> ELLIOTT
> (into radio)
> Single MAM, white shirt, dark
> tracksuit pants, building four,
> north-east corner.

CUT TO -

16.

23   **INT. HOUSE/UPSTAIRS MAIN ROOM - DAY**   23

- RAY.

Listening to ELLIOTT.

RAY is writing the details of the exchange in a notebook.

Once finished -

- there is silence again.

We start to hear noises of Ramadi city life.

A dog barking.

A motorbike passing.

Distant shouts.

Neighbours talking.

Extending through the house.

During this time -

- TOMMY appears from downstairs.

> TOMMY
> How is it, Dozer.

RAY pulls his headphones back.

> RAY
> Huh?

> TOMMY
> How's it going.

RAY isn't looking for a chat.

> RAY
> Yeah. Good.

TOMMY heads for the SNIPER ROOM.

24   **INT. HOUSE/SNIPER ROOM - DAY**   24

> FRANK
> My blue Nike hoodie has gone
> missing off the base. So if you
> see one of them wearing it, let me
> know.

17.

TOMMY enters. Takes a position by the PEACH CURTAINS.

                    FRANK (CONT'D)
How's it down there?

                    TOMMY
Cigarettes and tea. You want tea?

                    FRANK
Pass.

                    TOMMY
What have you got up here?

                    FRANK
Peekers.

                    TOMMY
Where.

                    FRANK
Corners of building four.

TOMMY heads for the window. Slightly pulls back the
curtains. Peeks out.

They fall back into silence.

25   **INT. HOUSE/UPSTAIRS MAIN ROOM - DAY**   25

RAY and ERIK sit in silence, for another minute.

RAY making notes.

26   **INT. HOUSE/UPSTAIRS KITCHEN-STORAGE - DAY**   26

DELETED

27   **INT. HOUSE/UPSTAIRS MAIN ROOM - DAY**   27

DELETED

28   **INT. HOUSE/MAIN BEDROOM - DAY**   28

DELETED

29   **INT. HOUSE/UPSTAIRS MAIN ROOM - DAY**   29

DOGS start barking.

ERIK rises.

ERIK moves to doorway of SNIPER ROOM.

CUT TO -

30   **INT. HOUSE/SNIPER ROOM - DAY**   30

- ELLIOTT.

>   ELLIOTT
> He's back.

>   FRANK
> White shirt?

>   ELLIOTT
> Yeah.

>   FRANK
> ... What do you want to do?

>   ELLIOTT
> Keep an eye on him.

CUT TO -

31   **INT. HOUSE/UPSTAIRS MAIN ROOM - DAY**   31

- RAY, writing.

ERIK - walks back into room - radios to JAKE.

JAKE is the Officer-in-Charge of OP-2.

After separating from OP-1 last night, OP-2 occupied another house. Storming it in the same way.

They now located are a few streets away.

>   ERIK
> Alpha 2, this is 1, we might have
> guys starting to move in on our
> position.

>   JAKE
>   (over radio)
> Maybe because they heard you
> sledging through that fucking wall
> all night. We could hear every
> strike. Why didn't you use a
> charge?

                              19.

                    ERIK
          Uh - didn't want to make a noise.

                    JAKE
                (over radio)
          Not sure that worked out for you.

CUT TO -

- RAY.

Getting up and moving to LT MACDONALD and SGT LAERRUS,
checking view on the laptop.

Changing frequency on his radio.

RAY is more conversational when talking to pilots. There is a
different, more formal etiquette on comms when talking to
military.

Then -

                    RAY
          Profane 5-4, Redman 6, can you slew
          your sensor west of my position,
          one-zero-zero metres, on building
          per GRG, call contact.

                    PROFANE 5-4
                (over radio)
          Yeah, zero 6. I contact.

                    RAY
          Hey, uh, we have an individual who
          was peeking on north-west corner of
          building four. He has disappeared
          to the west. Do you see anybody
          hanging around on that corner?
          Over.

                    PROFANE 5-4
                (over radio)
          Yes. A-ffirm. I contact that
          individual.

                    RAY
          Just be advised he has been probing
          our position. Do you see any
          massing or suspicious activity that
          would indicate a threat? Over.

                    PROFANE 5-4
                (over radio)
          Negative.
                    (MORE)

                    PROFANE 5-4 (CONT'D)
          Definitely a lot of civilians down
          there. I'll keep an eye on that
          sector for you.

                    RAY
          Roger that, Profane. Redman out.

INT. HOUSE/SNIPER ROOM - DAY   32

Back in the SNIPER ROOM.

ERIK RETURNS TO DOORWAY.

ELLIOTT focused on his scope.

                    ELLIOTT
          White shirt. Dark tracksuit pants.
          Fourth time he's done that.

                    FRANK
          Peeking or probing?

                    ELLIOTT
          Peeking with intent to probe.

                    FRANK
          How many times do we let this guy
          do this?

                    ELLIOTT
          I'm going to relay to OP-2.
               (into radio)
          Cowboy, give me a heads-up if you
          see this guy come to your position.
          White shirt, dark tracksuit pants.

                    COWBOY
               (over radio)
          Copy. We're getting a build-up of
          activity here too. I had a pair of
          guys in blue jeans, probing, twice.

                    ELLIOTT
          I have two MAMs of that
          description, just showed up here.
          Blue jeans, one red T-shirt.

                    COWBOY
               (over radio)
          Yeah, that's them.

21.

ELLIOTT
Looks like they're getting their
jihad on.

CUT TO -

INT. HOUSE/UPSTAIRS MAIN ROOM - DAY   33

33

- ERIK.

Listening to the OFFICER-IN-CHARGE of BRAVO - another platoon
elsewhere in Ramadi.

OIC BRAVO
(over radio)
Alpha 1, Bravo 1, we are in a TIC.
We're getting rockets and small-
arms fire. We're all good right
now but we're pulling air to our
position.

ERIK
(into radio)
Roger. Just check in with BDA when
able.

CUT TO RAY.

BRAVO FOUR
(over radio)
Alpha 5, this is Bravo 4. Hey, I
think we're going to need to pull
Profane to our AO. Over.

RAY
Roger, Bravo 4.

Then -

- the pilot flying air support comes in over the radio.

PROFANE 5-4
(over radio)
Redman 6, this Profane 5-4,
checking off station at this time.
Over.

RAY
Roger, Profane.

RAY comes off the radio.

                         RAY (CONT'D)
               Why are they pulling air from us
               and not sourcing it from somewhere
               else?

                         LT MACDONALD
               I'll check.

     SAM appears at the door to his room.

                         SAM
               What's up?

                         RAY
               We just lost air support. They
               pushed to Bravo.

                         SAM
               That's not good.

                         ERIK
               They are are troops in contact.

     SAM absorbing. Processing.

                         SAM
               Okay.

     SAM returns to his window.

34   **INT. HOUSE/MAIN BEDROOM - DAY**   34

     SAM takes position by the window.

35   **INT. HOUSE/UPSTAIRS MAIN ROOM - DAY**   35

     ONE MINUTE PASSES.

     ERIK SETTLES.

     Then -

     - a sudden BROADCAST starts from the minaret.

     It's loud.

     And it's speech.

     Non-musical. Not prayer.

     All the SEALS on the top floor of house hear it.

RAY, ERIK, ELLIOTT, FRANK, SAM.

They listen.

And know it doesn't feel right.

35A **INT. HOUSE/SNIPER ROOM - DAY** 35A

FRANK looks at ELLIOTT.

> FRANK
> Okay. That sucks.

> ELLIOTT

> It does.

> TOMMY
> I'll go see.

35B **INT. HOUSE/MAIN LIVING AREA - DAY** 35B

A few moments later -

- the sound of men coming up the stairs, quickly.

Both the two IRAQI SCOUTS, SIDAR and FARID appear.

They look scared.

ERIK appears at the doorway to the bedroom.

RAY and SAM stare at the IRAQI SCOUTS.

> SIDAR
> Captain Erik, Captain Erik. That's
> no good. No good.

> SAM
> What are they saying?

> SIDAR
> They are saying - we call on all
> Muslims for jihad.

RAY checks his watch.

Makes a note of the time.

Starts writing.

24.

> SIDAR (CONT'D)
> Jihad to come now. To kill you.
> Kill Americans.

ERIK hears it.

Doesn't like it.

But doesn't react much.

> ERIK
> Go keep lower deck locked down.

Neither SCOUT moves.

SAM points back at the stairs.

> SAM
> Downstairs. Keep it fucking
> secure.

The two SCOUTS exchange a glance.

Then head back down the stairs.

The broadcast suddenly stops.

SAM moves to ERIK.

> SAM (CONT'D)
> Think they're going to do it?

> ERIK
> We'll find out.

> SAM
> Yessir. Either way, we're locked
> on.

> ERIK
> Okay. You've been at it a while.
> Let's swap.

SAM and ERIK swap.

ERIK takes position by the window.

CUT TO -

36   **INT. HOUSE/UPSTAIRS MAIN ROOM - DAY**   36

- RAY, concentrating on the chatter coming in over his
headphones.

SAM sits next to RAY, where ERIK had been.

SAM offers RAY dip.

RAY takes it.

Uneasy silence between them.

CUT TO –

37   **INT. HOUSE/SNIPER ROOM – DAY**   37

– ELLIOTT, reaching in his pockets.

Pulling out dip – chewing tobacco.

The can is empty.

>   ELLIOTT
> Frank. Jump on this. I'm out of
> dip and need a stretch.

>   FRANK
> Yep.

FRANK taking over the rifle from ELLIOTT.

As FRANK settles on to the scope, ELLIOTT looks through his kit.

Finds a fresh can.

Stretches out the discomfort in his limbs.

FRANK scans through the scope.

>   FRANK (CONT'D)
> Yeah. We have definite massing.
>   (into radio)
> Six MAMs just exited building three
> in my sector.

>   COWBOY
>   (over radio)
> I'm seeing the same where we are.

TOMMY carefully peeks through the PEACH CURTAINS.

ELLIOTT taps FRANK.

FRANK comes off his rifle, and slides his legs over the edge of the table.

26.

Stands.

As ELLIOTT takes over -

- FRANK goes to the corner of the room and starts to piss into a bottle.

AT THAT MOMENT -

- there is a sudden flurry of movement, DIRECTLY outside the two holes that were knocked in the exterior walls.

Through the SNIPER HOLE - a dark defocused shape suddenly obscures the view.

Without anyone hearing or realising, Al-Qaeda fighters have crept onto their building via the rooftops -

- and are now ON the BALCONY.

Just outside the SNIPER room. Literally a few feet away from the soldiers.

The NEXT MOMENT -

- a GRENADE is simply pushed through the hole.

It hits the mesh/netting - which makes it fall directly downwards.

In front of ELLIOTT.

> ELLIOTT
> Grenade -

INSTINCTIVELY -

- ELLIOTT braces himself.

He drops his head, and clamps his arms to his sides.

TOMMY and FRANK both turn to the wall.

CUT TO -

38   **INT. HOUSE/UPSTAIRS MAIN ROOM - DAY**   38

- RAY and SAM.

Reacting as the GRENADE hits the floor of the SNIPER ROOM.

Hearing the distinctive METALLIC CLINKING sound as it lands.

                    SAM
                  (stunned)
              Fucking grenades -

RAY throws himself BACKWARDS.

Pulling his legs up.

Trying to roll into the room behind him.

BEFORE HE HAS COMPLETED THIS ACTION -

- there is a shockingly loud BANG, as the grenade EXPLODES.

Through the door to the SNIPER ROOM -

- the room erupts with grey smoke.

Debris and particles fly towards RAY.

THE NEXT MOMENT -

- gunfire starts.

When RAY lifts his head to look in the direction of the
SNIPER ROOM -

- through the hanging dust and smoke, he can see the PEACH
CURTAINS, that are drawn across the window.

They are dancing.

Flicking and plucking, as bullets fly through the material,
into the room.

The sight arrests him - momentarily.

CUT TO -

INT. HOUSE/SNIPER ROOM - DAY

- TOMMY.

He has been fragged. Small cuts.

He turns back from the wall.

Lifts his MK 48 MACHINE GUN and starts firing back through
the window.

Behind him, ELLIOTT has managed to exit the room.

FRANK is following ELLIOTT.

TOMMY is shuffle-footing with FRANK, continuing to fire.

CUT TO -

40   **INT. HOUSE/UPSTAIRS MAIN ROOM - DAY**   40

- RAY.

He starts CRAWLING FORWARDS towards his radio pack.

As RAY crawls forward -

- ERIK appears at the doorway to the MAIN BEDROOM.

- SAM picks himself up.

RAY gets to his radio.

As he starts strapping it on -

- FRANK and ELLIOTT start emerging from the SNIPER ROOM.

They are also crawling.

ELLIOTT is bleeding from somewhere on his arm. Blood is
streaming down his left hand as he pulls himself forwards.

AROUND RAY -

- ERIK is shouting from the doorway.

>   ERIK
>   Elliott - Frank - Tommy - you good?

None respond.

>   SAM
>   *Elliott!*

RAY pulls on his headphones -

- and immediately hears that OP-2, in their position a couple
of streets away, are ALSO being attacked.

Through the headphones, RAY can hear the loud crackle of
sustained gunfire.

>   JAKE
>   (over radio)
>   - our position under small-arms
>   fire -

RAY looks up and sees ELLIOTT.

ELLIOTT has got himself to the corner of the room.

FRANK is crouched beside him.

It's unclear whether FRANK is also injured.

RAY starts moving towards them.

As he does so -

- he looks to the METAL DOOR to the BALCONY.

Through the sliver of light, where the door is unable to close fully, RAY sees a dark shape pass across it.

>   RAY
>   MOVEMENT. BALCONY.

RAY starts firing, rolling the door, firing as he crosses it, directly through the metal.

He empties an entire magazine.

ERIK moves up to RAY'S position, and also fires through the metal door -

- as RAY reloads.

And continues firing.

Empties his entire second magazine.

In the aftermath from RAY firing in the room -

- it becomes clear that the gunfire from directly outside has stopped.

But now they can hear the slightly more distant gunfire from the firefight at OP-2's position.

CUT TO -

- FRANK.

Still crouched.

He looks dazed. Staring into space. Mentally locked out of what is happening around him.

CUT TO -

- ELLIOTT.

30.

He is lifting himself to a standing position, leaning against the wall.

He's staring at his hand.

Blood is streaming off his fingertips and splashing onto the floor.

He angry that he's been hit. And scared.

                    ELLIOTT
          Motherfucker. Fuck.

ERIK calls to ELLIOTT.

                    ERIK
          How bad is it?

                    ELLIOTT
          I'm okay.

SAM starts checking over ELLIOTT to make sure he's not critically hurt.

There's a lot of blood from ELLIOTT'S arm, but not an amount that would mean a vein had been cut.

SAM jokes to ELLIOTT, to calm him.

                    SAM
          Hey. You're going to get to see
          the girls of Charlie Med.

                    ERIK
          Sam?

                    SAM
          Yeah, he's okay. But we need to
          casevac him.

RAY starts radioing to HQ.

                    RAY
          This is Frogman-6 Romeo, we are
          troops in contact at our last known
          position. More info to follow.
          Stand by.

CONCURRENTLY -

- LT MACDONALD is also radioing in to get air support pulled back to them.

                    LT MACDONALD
          Wild Eagle base, Wild Eagle 2-4, we
          are troops in contact, requesting
          immediate air support.

SIDAR appears at the top of the stairwell, followed by FARID.

He looks around.

Sees ELLIOTT.

He looks extremely frightened. Eyes wide. Staring.

ERIK radios JAKE at OP-2.

                    ERIK
          Alpha 2. This is 1. We just had
          grenades thrown into our position.

ERIK is adrenalinised. In the hyper-aware state after a
contact has started.

                    JAKE
               (over radio)
          Copy, 1. We're in contact too.

                    ERIK
          Elliott is injured. Are we coming
          to you or are you coming to us?

                    JAKE
               (over radio)
          Stand by.

SAM looks round at the SCOUTS.

They are standing - looking dazed.

                    SAM
               (hard)
          Hey.

The SCOUTS look at SAM.

                    SAM (CONT'D)
          Get down there. Lock it down.

FARID and SIDAR go down the stairs.

                    RAY
          I think there's still dudes on our
          roof.

32.

ERIK is getting his head together. Making sure he speaks clearly.

>   ERIK
>   Okay. All OPs are under attack.
>   This mission is over. Here's what
>   we do. We're going to collapse to
>   the first deck and casevac Elliott.
>   Break it down. Let's get ready to
>   move.

LT MACDONALD and SGT LAERRUS start hurriedly packing their gear.

LT MACDONALD makes a move for the BALCONY DOOR.

SGT LAERRUS catches his arm.

>   SGT LAERRUS
>   Where you going?

>   LT MACDONALD
>   Got to go out. Get the receiver.

>   SGT LAERRUS
>   Bro. Not a good idea.

>   ERIK
>   No.

>   LT MACDONALD
>   ... Right.

LT MACDONALD starts winding in the cable, to drag the receiver through the METAL DOOR.

CONCURRENT WITH THIS —

— RAY relays to HQ.

>   RAY
>   (into radio)
>   Manchu, Frogman. We need a
>   casevac at our last known
>   position. Over.

>   MANCHU X-RAY
>   (over radio)
>   Confirm sector and building number.

>   RAY
>   (into radio)
>   OP-1 location as follows. Papa 1-0,
>   building 5-8. How copy.

                    MANCHU X-RAY
          Papa 1-0, building 5-8.

                    RAY
               (into radio)
          Good readback.

                    MANCHU X-RAY
               (over radio)
          Any amplifying remarks? Over.

RAY glances at ELLIOTT.

SAM is checking the wound on ELLIOTT'S arm.

                    RAY
          Negative. No amplifying remarks.
          Just casevac. Advise on ETA.
          Over.

                    MANCHU X-RAY
               (over radio)
          Roger that. Stand by. Over.

RAY starts getting his kit back on.

Vest chest-harness over his body-armour plate.

Helmet over his headphones.

CUT TO -

ELLIOTT.

He's starting to come round out of shock.

                    ELLIOTT
          Guys. My shit is still in there.

RAY looks round.

SAM is dealing with ELLIOTT'S wound.

                    RAY
          Where is it?

                    ELLIOTT
          I don't fucking know. It's in
          there somewhere.

                    RAY
          I'll grab it.

                              FRANK
                    My shit's in there too.

RAY moves to the doorway.

Peeks inside.

Sees -

- the PEACH CURTAINS, still hanging over the window.

Now pierced with bullet holes.

Everything else is chaos. The room looks completely
different.

Scorched. The tables are flipped over. Everything is piled
or shredded or covered in debris.

RAY takes a beat.

He doesn't want to go inside.

But although there is constant gunfire from OP-2's position,
there is no more gunfire from directly outside their
position.

RAY runs in.

41   **INT. HOUSE/SNIPER ROOM - DAY**   41

RAY hurriedly tries to search through the jumble of debris
and mats and rugs.

IN THE WHOLE COURSE OF THIS DAY -

- this is the moment RAY is aware of feeling the most fear.

He knows people are right outside the windows.

At any moment, he's expecting another burst of gunfire to
start punching in through the peach curtains.

He hunts around the debris, but he can't immediately find
ELLIOTT'S kit.

He just wants to get out of there.

42   **INT. HOUSE/UPSTAIRS MAIN ROOM - DAY**   42

ERIK hears JAKE at OP-2 the radio.

                    JAKE
              (over radio)
         Alpha 1, we're moving to you.
         We'll let you know when we're
         inbound.

                    ERIK
         Copy.

RAY exits back into the main room.

                    RAY
         I can't find shit. I don't know
         where the fuck it is.

                    ELLIOTT
         It's in there.

                    RAY
         I can't find it, bro.

HQ comes in over the radio.

                    MANCHU X-RAY
              (over radio)
         Frogman-6 Romeo, casevac is
         inbound. Callsign Bushmaster on ID
         7-5-5. ETA ten minutes. Over.

                    RAY
              (into radio)
         Copy. Bushmaster 7-5-5.

RAY relays to ERIK.

                    RAY (CONT'D)
         Bradley launched. ETA ten minutes.

                    ERIK
         Okay.
              (to platoon)
         Stack up. Get ready to collapse.
         We're moving down.

                    RAY
              (repeats)
         Sir, I think there's still guys on
         our building.

                    ERIK
         Sam - blow the Claymores as we
         move.

                    SAM
          Yessir.

                    ERIK
               (into radio)
          Alpha 2 - we'll be blowing
          Claymores.

                    JAKE
               (over radio)
          Affirm.

                    ELLIOTT
               (assertive)
          Guys, I need my shit. There's C-4
          in my backpack.

                    ERIK
          Yeah. I'll find it.

ERIK gestures to TOMMY.

                    ERIK (CONT'D)
          Tommy. Sam.

They both move to the door of the SNIPER ROOM.

TOMMY enters first.

Followed by ERIK and SAM.

TOMMY holds security while ERIK searches.

A few moments later, ERIK re-emerges with ELLIOTT'S pack,
HELMET, and RIFLE.

SAM helps ELLIOTT get his equipment on.

RAY assists.

Then the SEALS stack up, ready to move into the stairwell.

They arrange in this order - ERIK, ELLIOTT, FRANK, SAM, RAY.

As they position, SAM pulls out the trigger for the
CLAYMORES.

In a few seconds they are ready to go.

Then -

                    SAM
          Fire in the hole.

37.

CUT TO -

43   **<u>EXT. HOUSE/BALCONY - DAY</u>**   43

\- the CLAYMORES.

One beat.

Then they EXPLODE.

44   **<u>EXT. HOUSE - DAY</u>**   44

A massive detonation along the front face of the house.

45   **<u>INT. HOUSE/UPSTAIRS MAIN ROOM - DAY</u>**   45

The shockwave blows dust off the walls and floor.

It is as if the entire building and the ground beneath it
have jolted.

The scale of the explosion seems to take all the SEALS by
surprise - bigger and more extreme than they were expecting.

>   ERIK
>   (yells)
>   *Go, go.*

The SEALS start moving down the stairwell.

46   **<u>INT. HOUSE/HALL - DAY</u>**   46

The SEALS move off the stairs, into the HALL.

SIDAR is in with the IRAQI FAMILY.

The family look frozen in total confusion and horror as the
SEALS pass.

The daughters are crying. Panicking.

The MOTHER looks like she's screaming.

We can't hear her.

The family have dropped into a transcendent state of fear and
confusion.

The invasion, the grenades and the gunfire.

38.

The destruction of their home.

The deafening sound of the Claymores.

The blood splashing on the hall floor as ELLIOTT passes them.

47   **INT. HOUSE/KITCHEN - DAY**   47

The SEALS enter the KITCHEN.

TOMMY is holding his MACHINE GUN on the open front door.

FARID and the two Marines, LT MACDONALD and SGT LAERRUS, are with him.

A new voice comes in over RAY'S radio.

This is the driver of the BRADLEY FIGHTING VEHICLE - a tank with rear door that can been lowered, to allow easy access for troops.

The BRADLEY is the vehicle that has been sent for ELLIOTT'S medical evacuation.

>   BUSHMASTER 1
>   (over radio)
>   Frogman-6 Romeo, this is
>   Bushmaster. Your casevac is
>   inbound. We are seven minutes from
>   your position. Over.

>   RAY
>   Bushmaster, copy.
>   (to the SEALS)
>   Bradley ETA seven minutes.

>   ERIK
>   Okay.

ERIK radios JAKE.

>   ERIK (CONT'D)
>   (to Jake)
>   Alpha 2, we are prepping to receive
>   casevac. Are you guys broken down
>   yet?

Over JAKE'S radio, the distant firefight at OP-2 suddenly sounds extremely intense.

>   JAKE
>   (over radio)
>   Negative, 1. Not yet.

RAY taps ELLIOTT.

                    RAY
          You good?

ELLIOTT meets RAY'S gaze.

RAY and ELLIOTT are like brothers. Closer to each other than
they are to their actual families.

                    ELLIOTT
          Yeah, yeah. Good.

RAY nods.

ERIK addresses everyone.

                    ERIK
          Okay. Here's the breakout plan.
          Macadoo, Surreal - you're covering
          the family.

LT MACDONALD and SGT LAERRUS nod.

                    LT MACDONALD
          Yessir.

                    ERIK
          Ray, you're right here. When the
          tank rolls up, Frank pops smoke.
          The Iraqi scouts are going to lead
          us out. It's going to be Elliott,
          Sam, and I'm taking up the rear.
          Once Elliott gets in the tank,
          we're all going to come back
          inside the building.

                    SAM
          I'll get Elliott to the Cash.

RAY reacts.

The Cash is the Corps Area Support Hospital.

                    BUSHMASTER 1
                  (over radio)
          Frogman, this is Bushmaster.
          Advise on how to receive you.
          Over.

                                    40.

                    RAY
          Bushmaster, we will be extracting
          two pax, exiting from metal gate,
          directly outside our building.
          Over.

                    BUSHMASTER 1
                  (over radio)
          Copy, Frogman. Two pax, metal
          gate. ETA five minutes, over.

RAY relays.

                    RAY
          Tank five minutes.

ERIK radios to JAKE.

                    ERIK
          Alpha 2, we're going to breakout
          once the tank gets here. When we
          get Elliott evacuated, we're
          pulling back to our house. Once
          in our position, we're prepping to
          receive you. Is there anything we
          can do to facilitate your movement
          to us?

Again, when we hear JAKE, there is the backdrop of intense
GUNFIRE.

                    JAKE
                  (over radio)
          Just don't fucking shoot us when we
          roll up.

LT MACDONALD and SGT LAERRUS move to relieve SIDAR from
covering the IRAQI FAMILY.

SAM goes with them.

48   **INT. HOUSE/DOWNSTAIRS BEDROOM - DAY**   48

SAM enters the bedroom off the hall, with SIDAR and the IRAQI
family.

In a way, SIDAR looks as frightened as the family to see SAM.

                    SAM
                  (to Sidar)
          You, with me.

                    SIDAR
          ... Now?

41.

                          SAM
          Now.

SIDAR follows SAM.

LT MACDONALD and SGT LAERRUS take over from SIDAR.

The family stare at them, terrified.

There's nothing the two Marines can say to them.

CUT TO -

49   **INT. HOUSE/KITCHEN - DAY**   49

SAM enters the KITCHEN with SIDAR.

They pass FRANK - who is still in shock.

CUT TO -

- RAY.

OVER RAY'S HEADPHONES we hear a constant stream of chatter
between HQ, AIR SUPPORT, and JAKE at OP-2.

                          RADIO
                     (PROFANE 5-4)
                  - seeing group closing from north-
                  east of their position, count six
                  individuals -
                     (MANCHU X-RAY)
                  - Cash made aware and ready to
                  receive wounded -
                     (BUSHMASTER 1)
                  - three minutes out from their
                  position -
                     (JAKE)
                  - estimate we are ten minutes
                  behind, unable to breakout until -

As RAY listens -

- he watches SAM physically position the IRAQI SCOUTS in the
stack, lining them up in the lead position ahead of ELLIOTT.

He notices how scared the SCOUTS are.

The fear is partly in their posture. The way they are
hunched forwards, as if expecting something about to surprise
them from behind. The way they are tightly gripping their AK-
47s.

It's also in their behaviour. They talk rapidly in Arabic to each other. But when SAM talks to them, it is as if they are looking through him. Not quite hearing or understanding. Overwhelmed by the inputs and the confusion.

                    BUSHMASTER 1
               (over radio)
          Frogman, we are two mikes. Over.

                    RAY
          Tank is two minutes out.

                    OP-1
          Two minutes.

A moment of silence, as -

- through the crackle of gunfire from OP-2's position, they start to hear -

- the distinctive grinding sound of a TANK ENGINE.

                    ERIK
          I hear it. Frank - prep the smoke.

FRANK takes one HEAVY-CONCEALMENT SMOKE GRENADE from his belt.

Steps closer to the FRONT ENTRANCE, beside the stack.

The TANK ENGINE is getting louder.

The SEALS do final checks.

                    RAY
          Tank is one minute.

                    OP-1
          One minute.

                    ERIK
          Frank. Smoke out.

FRANK steps to the ENTRANCE DOOR.

He pulls the pin from the SMOKE GRENADE.

Throws it.

But wherever it lands -

- it evidently hasn't been thrown quite far enough.

Within seconds -

43.

- the COURTYARD directly outside the front entrance has filled with dense white smoke.

And moments later, the smoke starts ROLLING IN to the kitchen through the open FRONT ENTRANCE DOOR.

> SAM
> Fuck -

Chaos starting to descend.

Visibility clouding.

Everyone starts coughing.

Through the coughing -

- we hear the TANK arrive.

> RAY
> *Tank is here.*

> ERIK
> *Breakout, breakout, breakout.*

SAM physically drives the IRAQI SCOUTS forward.

> SAM
> *Go, go, go.*

The STACK moves out through the door.

RAY loses sight of them into the smoke.

The situation doesn't feel right.

He wants to get eyes on them.

He hesitates a moment.

Then follows.

50   **EXT. HOUSE/COURTYARD - DAY**   50

RAY steps into the courtyard.

In the dense white smoke -

- he glimpses the shadow shape of ERIK.

Then ERIK vanishes again.

RAY moves to the edge of the courtyard.

Around the cover of the HIGH WALL, to the start of the DRIVEWAY.

As he peers into the smoke, trying to see the others -

CUT TO -

51   **EXT. HOUSE/DRIVEWAY - DAY**   51

- the STACK, moving down the DRIVEWAY.

Bunched up - hardly able to see each other.

The TANK ENGINE is LOUD.

SIDAR and FARID reach the METAL GATE.

They pull it open.

They step through -

- onto the road.

52   **EXT. ROAD - DAY**   52

On the road, the smoke is slightly thinner.

The SCOUTS see -

- the BRADLEY FIGHTING VEHICLE TANK, pulled up just to the right of the gate, is facing the building.

The REAR RAMP is open, ready to receive ELLIOTT.

Through the open hatch, they can see the legs of the TANK GUNNER, standing up in his gun hatch.

SIDAR goes left, to give cover.

FARID goes right, towards the TANK.

ELLIOTT follows directly behind.

He steps into the road.

SAM is just behind ELLIOTT, at the metal gate.

ERIK is a few steps behind SAM, still in the driveway.

Then -

- an IED explodes.

Hidden at some point, just to the left of the gate.

Perhaps during the night.

Perhaps in the morning, shortly before the house was attacked.

It is a huge explosion.

It rips out directly along the ground, at waist-height.

The IED is a high-level, expertly constructed device. Of the sort provided to insurgent forces by Iran and Syria.

Aside from the explosive charge, the IED contains metal shrapnel and white phosphorus. It spreads chunks of fiercely burning material into the area, and anyone in it.

FARID is blown in half. His body is completely destroyed, just below the ribcage.

His chest, shoulders, arms, and head remain in one piece, and land a few feet from where he was standing.

ELLIOTT is caught in the legs.

Below the knee area, both legs are extremely badly damaged. Bones are shattered. Muscle is shredded. Below the knee, only sinews and strips of flesh hold his legs and feet together.

SAM catches similar damage, but only in his right leg.

CUT TO -

53   **EXT. HOUSE/DRIVEWAY - DAY**   53

- RAY.

Caught in the shockwave of the explosion.

He is thrown backwards.

Hits the wall of the house.

Is knocked unconscious.

CUT TO -

54   **EXT. ROAD - DAY**   54

- the road.

SUDDENLY BLACK.

As if the sun has been taken out of the sky. Dark with the hanging dust and smoke.

As gunfire suddenly erupts.

Shooting, from no clear locations.

Bullets start to hit the TANK.

Through the open rear doors, we can see the TANK GUNNER.

Somehow, he has been wounded in the leg.

CUT TO -

55   **EXT. HOUSE/DRIVEWAY - DAY**   55

- IN THE DARKNESS, somewhere in the courtyard, TOMMY lies unconscious.

His eyes flutter.

Through his daze, he can hear SAM SCREAMING.

> SAM
> OH MY GOD. OH MY GOD.

CUT TO -

- IN THE DARKNESS, somewhere in the courtyard, ERIK lies unconscious.

ERIK comes to.

He is dazed.

There is a strange yellow hue to the darkness.

He takes a lungful of air.

The air is so hot that it literally burns his oesophagus.

There is also a chemical stench in the air. It feels poisonous. Sharp, acrid, toxic.

He has no choice but to breathe it in.

He feels pain in his chest, as if his lungs are being torn out.

SOMEWHERE IN THE DARKNESS -

- SAM'S words become screaming.

No words. Desperate, animal screams.

Continuous.

ERIK starts crawling forward, towards the screaming.

He moves through the gate.

56 **INT. ROAD - DAY** 56

ERIK crawls into the road.

He sees -

- the shape of the BRADLEY through the smoke and dust.

The top half of one of the Iraqi scouts.

ELLIOTT, lying a little distance away.

Nearer, SAM. Screaming.

Both SAM and ELLIOTT seem to be on fire.

Their legs seem to be lying in the wrong direction.

ERIK crawls to SAM.

Reaches him.

Starts patting out the fire with his hands.

One of SAM'S feet looks like it's about to fall off.

ERIK starts to drag SAM while crawling.

Then stands, to pull him.

He gets him through the gate.

CUT TO -

- the BRADLEY.

The rear doors start to rise.

The TANK starts to move.

In a few seconds, it is gone.

The street is empty except for the bodies of the dead and wounded.

Smoke drifts through the scene.

The sound of the TANK engine fades.

The noise of gunfire continues.

SIDAR picks himself up.

He is streaked in blood. Wounded.

But he manages to get to his feet. And then start to run.

57   **EXT. HOUSE/DRIVEWAY - DAY**   57

- RAY.

He is lying unconscious.

Half propped up against the wall. Tipped over to his side.

Beats pass.

Then -

- RAY wakes with a jolt.

Sudden awareness.

He can see almost nothing in the smoke.

From somewhere, he can hear SAM screaming.

RAY gets up.

He starts to move towards where he knows the METAL GATE must be.

He sees no one.

No dark shapes or figures in the smoke.

He moves again.

Then stops.

Suddenly aware he might run into the gate.

He steps forwards.

Holds his hands out.

Sees the gate.

Gets a hand to it.

CUT TO -

58   **EXT. HOUSE/DRIVEWAY - DAY**   58

- TOMMY getting to his feet.

Confused.

Staggering.

He moves back towards the air bricks.

Stops at the wall.

Turns back.

Lifts his gun - and fires a few rounds. Angled up, roughly
towards the buildings opposite. Almost blindly into the
smoke.

59   **EXT. ROAD - DAY**   59

RAY steps into the road.

The sound of SAM screaming has inexplicably stopped.

There is no sound.

He walks past the top section of FARID'S body.

Clumps of burning phosphorus are spread on the ground.

Wind is blowing.

It is sporadically clearing and returning the smoke from the
driveway.

Revealing and hiding the street.

RAY sees -

- ELLIOTT.

He's lying a few feet away.

Aside from his shattered legs, his arm is broken.

He is covered in a thick layer of dirt, from head to toe.

Beneath the dirt, blood is oozing, like water pushing up from beneath dry soil.

He has been burned.

Pellets of burning phosphorus are still embedded in his body.

The metal casing of his bullet magazines, strapped to his torso, have been curved by the force of the explosion.

Just above the curved magazines, the thick antennae on his radio has been sheared off.

RAY stares at ELLIOTT.

RAY'S chin starts to tremble, like a kid on the verge of tears.

                    RAY
          No - no - no - no -

RAY can't move.

His mind is completely emotionally overloaded. Overwhelmed.

The surge of inputs are too extreme.

RAY is locked into this frozen state.

Seconds pass.

Ten seconds.

Twenty.

Thirty.

The time passing feels stretched.

Infinite.

Then -

- RAY starts to hear a SNAPPING SOUND.

It is the sounds of bullets breaking the sound barrier.

Passing nearby.

Then he becomes aware of bullet impacts.

Rounds, kicking up dust as they hit the ground.

Hit the wall.

He realises -

- the impacts are everywhere.

Around the whole area.

Automatically, RAY lifts his rifle.

He returns fire across the street.

At the rooftops. The windows.

Ten or fifteen rounds.

Then he moves into action.

He reaches down, and finds ELLIOTT'S grab handle - the handle attached to a soldier's backpack, providing a grip so they can be dragged.

As he drags ELLIOTT -

- RAY'S hearing and awareness of his environment is growing more acute.

The sound of the gunshots becomes louder, and more penetrating.

As they grow louder, they become more alarming.

The emotional overload of seeing ELLIOTT, and the post-concussion daze, is being replaced with awareness, and the sense of self-preservation.

In addition, RAY starts to become aware of the RADIO CHATTER coming over his headphones, coming from TANK, HQ, and AIR SUPPORT.

The noise has been there the whole time. But he hasn't been hearing it.

FROM NOW UNTIL RAY REMOVES HIS HEADPHONES, THERE IS A CONSTANT BACKDROP OF RADIO CHATTER.

And to COMPOUND THE SENSE OF NIGHTMARE -

- at EXACTLY the rate that RAY'S awareness, alarm, and sense of urgency is growing -

- he is slowing down, increasingly struggling with the weight of ELLIOTT'S body.

Dragging a man of ELLIOTT'S size is exhausting in a way that adrenalin can't override.

RAY'S legs are burning. He's breathing hard, but can't get enough oxygen into his system.

Eventually he is only managing to drag ELLIOTT a single step at a time.

Between breaths, RAY starts shouting.

> RAY (CONT'D)
> *On me. One on me. Give me one.*

It's a call for help.

No one comes.

Eventually -

- he manages to get ELLIOTT to the end of the DRIVEWAY.

But as he pulls ELLIOTT into the courtyard, around the cover of the HIGH WALL with ventilating air bricks -

- ELLIOTT'S legs catch on something.

The shredded parts of his lower legs have hooked around the corner of the wall.

He is stuck - part in cover, half out.

RAY can't pull harder without the risk of tearing ELLIOTT'S lower legs off.

And he can't go back around the wall and free the legs without re-exposing himself to the gunfire.

RAY releases ELLIOTT'S drag handle.

Then goes back to the FRONT ENTRANCE of the house.

60   **INT. HOUSE/KITCHEN - DAY**   60

When RAY appears in the front entrance, he is initially confused by the sight in front of him.

SAM is lying on the kitchen floor, and ERIK is trying to give SAM first aid.

ERIK is simultaneously talking into his comms.

His voice sounds hoarse through his burned throat.

But though he sounds winded and dazed, we can hear the overwhelming sense of urgency in his voice.

>   ERIK
>   (into radio)
>   Jake - we just got slammed. We got
>   hit really bad. We've taken
>   massive casualties. Anticipating
>   coordinated enemy attack on our
>   position at any moment. We need
>   you to collapse to us. Time, now.

One of SAM'S legs seems unscathed. But the other, the right leg, is damaged very similarly to ELLIOTT. Brutally torn apart below the knee.

FRANK is standing on the other side of the room.

TOMMY is standing where he was left, theoretically covering the entrance with his machine gun.

But TOMMY is not watching the entrance. Nor is FRANK.

They are both staring at SAM'S leg. Eyes like saucers.

Then -

- sensing the figure in the doorway, TOMMY turns.

He shifts his wide-eyed stare from SAM'S leg to RAY.

But he says nothing.

Beat.

>   RAY
>   ... What are you doing?

TOMMY doesn't reply.

>   RAY (CONT'D)
>   (harder)
>   What are you *doing*? I need you to
>   *help* me. Get the fuck *out* here.

TOMMY moves towards RAY.

EXT. HOUSE/COURTYARD - DAY   61

TOMMY sees ELLIOTT, lying at the edge of the wall.

>   RAY
>   *Cover high, cover high.*

TOMMY'S training kicks in.

He moves up to the corner of the wall, by ELLIOTT'S body.

Swings his machine gun up, sweeping the rooftops.

RAY ducks around the corner of the wall, out into the open.

He frees the bloody tangle of ELLIOTT'S legs, where they had snagged on the bricks.

> RAY (CONT'D)
> Get his grab handle.

TOMMY gets a hold of the handle.

RAY holds Elliott's legs - gripping them by the material of his pants, behind the knees.

Then they start carrying ELLIOTT back towards the house.

62 **INT. HOUSE/KITCHEN - DAY** 62

TOMMY and RAY pull ELLIOTT into the kitchen and lay him out beside SAM.

LT MACDONALD has entered to assist ERIK.

SGT LAERRUS has appeared at the door to the hall.

ERIK is talking to SAM, but RAY can't hear what he's saying.

RAY becomes aware of the RADIO NOISE through his headphones.

He disconnects his radio on his chest -

- and the CONSTANT CHATTER abruptly stops.

Now RAY can hear the room around him.

SAM is making a loud, continuous moaning noise.

ERIK is talking.

> ERIK
> (into radio)
> Alpha 2, Alpha 1 - I need you move
> to us now -

> JAKE
> (over radio)
> I'm tracking but where are you
> guys.

                              ERIK
                        (into radio)
                You look for the blood and smoke.

CUT TO -

RAY starts trying to give ELLIOTT a head-to-toe sweep, to
assess his injuries.

But there's dirt and torn muscle everywhere.

He's completely soaked in blood.

He tries to check for a PULSE on ELLIOTT'S neck but feels
nothing.

And when he starts cutting ELLIOTT'S gear off, RAY finds a
hole in ELLIOTT'S shoulder, the size of a softball.

It's impossible to know where to start.

Then -

- the assessment is SUDDENLY interrupted -

- as bullets start striking the outside wall of the building.

And the NEXT MOMENT -

- a sequence of GRENADES start detonating.

The explosions are in the COURTYARD and DRIVEWAY.

Just a few feet away.

The noise and concussion of the detonations is overwhelming.

They are hammer-blows of brutalising shocks.

CUT TO -

- ERIK.

Instinctively hunching with each explosion.

AT THIS MOMENT, and FROM HERE ON, something in ERIK changes.

Aside from shock and toxic smoke inhalation, ERIK is
suffering from the effects of CONCUSSION.

He seems part-dissociated from the events around him - as if
thoughts and actions are having to penetrate through a fog.

CUT TO –

– RAY.

Through the deafening noise, he finds himself shouting:

> RAY
> *Two rooms deep. Two rooms deep.*
> *Go, go.*

It's a piece of entrenched memory training, kicking in.

The soldiers react.

They start trying to drag SAM and ELLIOTT deeper into the house, to the hall.

ERIK and LT MACDONALD try to pick up SAM.

RAY and TOMMY pick up ELLIOTT.

But ERIK and LT MACDONALD struggle with SAM'S dead weight.

And as soon as they lift him, his moaning becomes SCREAMING.

RAY moves to help them with SAM.

They carry him through –

63   **INT. HOUSE/HALL – DAY**   63

– to the HALL.

And lay him out.

NOTE – that RAY is ALSO suffering from shock and concussion.

For him, it takes a different form to ERIK.

Rather than dissociation, he experiences powerful SURGES, alternating between –

– AWARENESS of what is happening, with CLEAR THINKING.

– a state of being TOTALLY OVERWHELMED, similar to the frozen moment in the road, when he first saw ELLIOTT'S body.

It is as if his mind becomes so filled with inputs and processes and the extremeness of the situation that he slips into a DAZE.

Inside the daze, he has no knowledge that he has stopped functioning for a few moments.

It is only when he 'wakes' from the state that he realises he has drifted. Each time he 'wakes', he feels a strange sense of surprise - *what just happened?*

ONE OF THESE DAZE STATES HAPPENS NOW.

RAY is kneeling by SAM'S body.

ERIK is on the other side of SAM'S body.

Looking around at something. As if distracted.

SAM is screaming, but inaudible.

BEHIND ERIK - the Iraqi BROTHER from upstairs is shouting.

SGT LAERRUS is trying to calm him.

The moment extends.

Then -

- RAY 'wakes'.

And finds that -

- ELLIOTT has been carried through to the HALL, and is lying at the feet of SAM.

LT MACDONALD and TOMMY are with him.

TOMMY then takes up position by the hall entrance.

SAM has stopped screaming, and is moaning again.

SGT LAERRUS is covering the door to the IRAQI FAMILY.

RAY clicks back into gear.

He activates his comms.

> RAY
> Manchu-6 X-Ray, this is Frogman-6
> Romeo.

There is no response over the radio.

> RAY (CONT'D)
> Manchu-6 X-Ray, this is Frogman-6
> Romeo.

No response again.

RAY realises that he shut down his radio when he started to assess ELLIOTT in the kitchen.

He reconnects -

- and suddenly he can hear JAKE is talking. Gunfire in background again.

But now that they are deeper inside the house, the RADIO SIGNAL is bad. Intermittent.

> JAKE
> - for OP-1 position - we are in contact, will be breaking out hot in -

RAY switches channel.

> RAY
> Manchu-6 X-Ray, this is Frogman-6 Romeo. We have taken two casualties. We're going to need another casevac as soon as possible. Be advised there was an IED that caused the injuries. Over.

> MANCHU X-RAY
> (over radio, bad signal)
> Frogman, say again.

> RAY
> Manchu-6 X-Ray, this is Frogman-6 Romeo. We have two severely wounded. We need another casevac. Over.

SAM has heard this exchange.

It's the first words we've heard him speak since his leg was half-blown off.

> SAM
> (panicking)
> Who's the severely wounded?

SAM has no understanding of the state of his leg.

> RAY
> It's not you.

> SAM
> But who is it?

                    RAY
          Sam - not you. Don't worry about
          it.

                    SAM
          Is it me?

                    RAY
          No. No way. You're all good.

                    MANCHU X-RAY
               (over radio, bad signal)
          Frogman, understand two casualties.

                    RAY
          Be advised of IED, over.

                    MANCHU X-RAY
               (over radio, bad signal)
          Roger that. Stand by. Over.

RAY looks over at ELLIOTT.

ELLIOTT is lying motionless, on his back, as if dead.

He has given no sign of life since being found in the road.

TOMMY is standing beside ELLIOTT -

- but is doing nothing. He's just kneeling there.

The sight of ELLIOTT starts to overwhelm RAY. It's too hard
for him to look at.

RAY looks away.

LT MACDONALD is trying get his shit together, and work out
what he can do to be helpful.

He takes in the scene. The chaos and blood, and confusion.

He finds himself speaking.

                    LT MACDONALD
          Hey. We've got air back. We can't
          do gun runs because the bad guys
          are right on top of us. But we can
          coordinate a show of force. Do you
          want me to do it?

                    RAY
          Do it.

                    LT MACDONALD
                     (into radio)
              Profane 54, Wild Eagle 24,
              requesting immediate show of force
              our position, over our position
              OP-1, from east to west.

As LT MACDONALD is radioing in, RAY turns to SAM.

To his LEG.

Training gives him an action to carry out.

RAY reaches into his med-kit, and pulls out GAUZE.

He starts attempting to dress SAM'S wound.

But the blood immediately saturates the material. It's
useless.

                        RAY
              I need more gauze.

Beat.

                    RAY (CONT'D)
              ... Guys. I need more gauze.

Someone hands him another dressing.

He applies it -

- and the same thing happens.

The GAUZE is useless.

Pointless.

And as RAY stares at it -

- there is a sudden, rushing, ROAR of DEAFENING NOISE.

It is a FIGHTER JET passing very low, directly over their
position.

The jet is doing a SHOW OF FORCE - deliberately using the
sound of the engines to intimidate enemy attackers - and
making them believe a bombing run might be about to start.

When the jet has passed, and the STUNNING BLAST of NOISE has
subsided -

- RAY has sunk back into a DAZE STATE.

He is zoned in on SAM'S wound.

The drenched useless dressing.

The way the leg is almost hanging off.

The blood, that has entirely soaked SAM below the waist.

Moments pass.

Noises blur.

Become tone.

The moment extends.

And extends.

Then -

- in a RUSH, as if ALL SENSES RETURNING AT ONCE -

- RAY snaps back into focus.

He looks up from SAM.

Jabs a finger at SGT LAERRUS.

> RAY (CONT'D)
> *Hey. Bro.* I need you to take over
> comms for me.

> SGT LAERRUS
> ... Okay. I got it.

RAY looks to FRANK.

Sees -

- FRANK is standing at the side of the room.

Beside him, the IRAQI FAMILY are in the same room they have been held in since the previous night.

No one is securing the FAMILY any more, but they aren't moving.

Their expressions are beyond fear. It is more as if, in a literal way, they can't believe or comprehend what is happening.

RAY shouts at FRANK.

                         RAY
              Frank.

FRANK doesn't react.

                         RAY (CONT'D)
              Frank.

FRANK hears.

                         RAY (CONT'D)
              Lock the fucking stairwell down.
              There's guys up there.

FRANK moves off the wall.

On training autopilot.

64   **INT. HOUSE/STAIRS - DAY**   64

FRANK enters the stairwell, and brings his weapon up to cover
the entry point.

CUT TO -

65   **INT. HOUSE/HALL - DAY**   65

- SGT LAERRUS.

                    SGT LAERRUS
          Wild Eagle base, this Wild Eagle 2-
          6, requesting you push air support
          over our grid at this time. We are
          receiving small-arms fire,
          grenades. Two severely wounded.
          We need air support. Over.

                   WILD EAGLE BASE
              (over radio, bad signal)
          Roger that. Stand by.

CUT TO -

- LT MACDONALD moving to kneel beside ELLIOTT.

He does an injury survey. Aside from the terrible damage to
ELLIOTT'S legs, he finds wounds everywhere, including bad
shrapnel injuries ELLIOTT'S lower abdomen.

CUT TO -

- RAY, starting cutting away the material of SAM'S pants.

As soon as RAY starts doing this, SAM starts screaming.

> SAM
> NO, NO, NO! DON'T, DON'T! NO, NO -

The words become unintelligible.

Just continuous screaming.

RAY rips away the material.

SAM isn't wearing underwear.

Blood is pouring from somewhere on SAM'S upper leg.

RAY moves SAM'S penis, looking for the wound.

SAM continues to scream.

RAY finds a U-SHAPED WOUND on SAM'S thigh.

It's bleeding profusely - a major source of SAM'S blood loss, above the knee.

SAM starts begging.

> SAM (CONT'D)
> Please - just stop.

> RAY
> Sam - I've got to get a tourniquet
> on you.

> SAM
> No, don't. Don't touch me.

> RAY
> Sam -

> SAM
> No - Ray, don't. Just please don't
> touch my leg any more.

> RAY
> I've got to.

> SAM
> *No - no. Don't touch me. No, no,*
> *no.*

CONCURRENT TO THIS -

- LT MACDONALD is talking to ELLIOTT, even though ELLIOTT is giving no sign of being conscious.

64.

> LT MACDONALD
> Hey, bro - someone's here,
> someone's helping you. You just
> hang in there. I've got you. I'm
> pretty sure your leg is not good,
> but I'm going to get a tourniquet
> on. It's coming over your boot
> now.

As he talks, he is trying to get a tourniquet to slide up one
of ELLIOTT'S incredibly damaged legs. But it's impossible.

> LT MACDONALD (CONT'D)
> Okay - okay bro, this isn't going
> to work. Your leg's like a tree
> trunk, man. I'm going to
> disassemble this. Do it that way.

CUT TO -

- RAY.

Finding a tourniquet in his med-kit.

CUT TO -

- SGT LAERRUS, radioing in to HQ FSO - Fire Support Officer.

> SGT LAERRUS
> Wild Eagle base, have air asset
> check in with 2-6 on this freq,
> over.

> WILD EAGLE BASE
> .(over radio, bad signal)
> Roger. Be advised Profane 5-6 and
> 5-7, ETA three minutes. Over.

> SGT LAERRUS
> Roger that. Standing by. Over.

MEANWHILE -

- RAY has pulled the TOURNIQUET from his med-kit.

The tourniquet is essentially a fat canvas belt, that needs
to be fed into a BRASS BUCKLE.

But when RAY tries to feed it through -

- he finds that his fingers are not working properly. They
feel clumsy.

It's an obscure effect of being in shock - losing fine motor skills.

And it is another of the moments that feel like they belong in a nightmare.

A simple action: feeding a belt into a buckle.

The action being a literal matter of life and death.

Wanting to do it.

Needing to do it.

But being unable.

Each time RAY tries, the material folds against the buckle, and fails to push through.

And the entire time, SAM is moaning in pain, and blood is continuing to pour out from his shattered leg, and the U-shaped wound in his thigh.

BESIDE RAY -

- ERIK watches.

                    RAY
          Fuck.

RAY glazes for a beat.

He is starting to drop into a DAZE again.

But he pulls out of it.

Makes a decision.

He speaks to SAM.

                    RAY (CONT'D)
          Hey -

                    SAM
          No -

                    RAY

          - I'm going to do something. It's
          going to hurt.

SAM starts to panic.

                    SAM
          No, Ray, don't -

RAY starts to lift himself up slightly.

                    RAY
          I need to do this -

                    SAM
          - Ray, don't fucking touch me -
          don't fucking touch me - don't -

RAY pulls himself over SAM'S body -

- and jams his knee down on SAM'S thigh. Putting his weight
onto it. Using the weight as a form of tourniquet until he
can get the buckle threaded.

SAM starts screaming.

High. Loud. Continuous.

It doesn't stop.

RAY ZONES OUT.

CUT TO -

66   **<u>INT. HOUSE/STAIRS - DAY</u>**   66

- FRANK on the stairs.

Gun trained at the doorway to the upstairs room.

SAM screaming.

CUT TO -

67   **<u>INT. HOUSE/DOWNSTAIRS BEDROOM - DAY</u>**   67

- the IRAQI FAMILY.

The MOTHER trying to cover her daughter's ears and sight.

The MAN sitting on the edge of the bed.

SAM screaming.

CUT TO -

68   **<u>EXT. ROAD - DAY</u>**   68

- what is left of FARID'S body, in the empty road.

67.

The bright sun.

The distant crackle of OP-2's gunfight in the background.

SAM'S screaming slightly quieter, coming from inside the house.

CUT TO -

69   <u>**INT. HOUSE/HALL - DAY**</u>   69

- SAM screaming.

CUT TO -

- RAY.

Coming back into focus.

Seeing -

- ERIK.

Cranking the TOURNIQUET over SAM'S leg.

RAY gets off SAM'S leg.

SAM stops screaming.

Starts moaning.

And the NEXT MOMENT -

- behind RAY, ELLIOTT SUDDENLY WAKES.

He comes round seemingly instantly.

From apparently dead, to howling with pain. Just like SAM.

RAY'S head snaps around.

Stunned that ELLIOTT is alive.

Then -

- through his screams, words start emerging from ELLIOTT'S mouth.

> ELLIOTT
> *I need morphine. Morphine. Give*
> *me morphine.*

RAY and LT MACDONALD, who is with ELLIOTT, lock eyes.

                    ELLIOTT (CONT'D)
          Give me morphine, GIVE ME MORPHINE.

RAY turns to ERIK.

                    RAY
          Sir - what should we do?

ERIK looks blank.

                    ERIK
          What?

                    RAY
          Do we give him morphine? He's lost
          a lot of blood.

                    ERIK
          I don't know, man. It could kill
          him.

                    RAY
          ... So what should we do?

                    ERIK
          ... I don't know.

ELLIOTT'S screaming becomes moaning.

                    ELLIOTT
          Give me morphine, give me morphine,
          give me morphine -

                    RAY
          Fuck.

RAY turns back to LT MACDONALD.

                    RAY (CONT'D)
          Give it to him.

                    LT MACDONALD
          I don't know where the morphine is.

Amazingly, ELLIOTT finds the ability to speak calmly.

                    ELLIOTT
          It's in my bag. Medic bag. The
          pocket.

ELLIOTT'S pack is still strapped to his back.

It's under him.

                    LT MACDONALD
          Okay, okay - getting it -

LT MACDONALD starts trying to reach under ELLIOTT, to get to
his bag.

He gets the pack open.

Starts dragging stuff out.

SAM, through his fog of pain, has heard ELLIOTT.

                         SAM
          Ray. I need morphine too. You've
          got to give me some.

LT MACDONALD locates the morphine injectors.

They work like epipens - pushed against the skin, a needle
shoots out and delivers a dose.

                    LT MACDONALD
          Okay - I got them.

                         SAM
          Give me the morphine, Ray. I'm
          dying.

                         RAY
          You're not dying. You're not that
          bad. You're good.

                         SAM
          I'm dying. Just give me it.

                       ELLIOTT
          *Give me morphine. Give me
          morphine.*

LT MACDONALD looks at RAY.

He's holding the injectors. Waiting for the order.

                         RAY
          Do it.

LT MACDONALD hands one of the INJECTORS to ERIK.

Then he takes the other.

Preps it.

Lifts it.

And jams it into ELLIOTT'S leg.

Then yanks his hand back - as if he's been stung.

In his hurry, or panic, LT MACDONALD has held the INJECTOR the wrong way round -

- and has injected morphine into his own thumb.

> LT MACDONALD
> Ah - shit - shit -

LT MACDONALD feels a sudden shift inside himself, as the morphine enters his system.

ELLIOTT cries out on pain.

> SGT LAERRUS
> Are you fucked now?

> LT MACDONALD
> No - I'm good.

> ELLIOTT
> Bro. I need the morphine.

> LT MACDONALD
> Right - the first one - uh - it
> didn't work.

> ELLIOTT
> Get another.

> LT MACDONALD
> Right.

> ELLIOTT
> Do it in my arm.

LT MACDONALD grabs another INJECTOR -

- and successfully doses ELLIOTT.

It has an almost immediate effect - just taking the edge off ELLIOTT'S pain and fear.

His half-screams soften into moans.

CUT TO -

- ERIK and RAY.

They've just watched what happened.

ERIK looks down at the INJECTOR in his palm.

He can feel the way concussion is slowing his thinking.

He looks at RAY.

And shakes his head - as if to say: I can't do it.

Then he holds the injector out to RAY.

> ERIK
> ... Here.

A beat.

Then RAY takes it.

He focused carefully.

Makes sure it's the right way round.

Then jams SAM in the leg.

SAM'S screams also soften.

He starts talking again. And he's calmer.

RAY starts applying GAUZE to the U-shaped wound on SAM'S leg.

As he works, SAM watches him.

Then speaks.

> SAM
> I need more morphine.

> RAY
> We can't give you more.

> SAM
> Just give more. It's not enough.

> RAY
> It will kill you, man.

> SAM
> *It's not enough!*

> RAY
> *Hey.* You can't have more. Just
> chill the fuck out. You're going
> to be okay. You're not dying, and
> your junk is still there.

                    SAM
          But my feet are gone.

                    RAY
          They're not gone, bro. They're
          just in the wrong place. I'm
          telling you, you're good, man.
          You're not the one we're worried
          about. Breathe. Stay calm.

SAM relaxes slightly.

                    RAY (CONT'D)
          The boys are coming to us. You're
          good.

AS THEY TALK -

- unnoticed by RAY, ERIK stands.

The CONCUSSION is overwhelming him.

He walks towards the room with the IRAQI FAMILY.

70   **INT. HOUSE/DOWNSTAIRS BEDROOM - DAY**   70

ERIK enters the room with the IRAQI family.

The MAN is still sat on the edge of the bed.

The MOTHER is on the bed with the two GIRLS.

They look back at ERIK.

Not knowing why he has entered, or what is about to happen.

THEN -

- all sound is obliterated by a rapid build, then ROAR of JET
ENGINES. A second SHOW OF FORCE by a FIGHTER JET.

Again, NOISE fills the house entirely.

CUT TO -

71   **INT. HOUSE/HALL - DAY**   71

- RAY.

The NOISE of the JET has pushed RAY back in dissociation.

This dissociation is more extreme than the previous times.

73.

All awareness of environment drops out for RAY, except the enveloping NOISE.

When the sound of the jet subsides –

– there is the sound of GUNFIRE from outside.

CUT TO –

72 **EXT. ROAD – DAY**   72

– the soldiers of OP-2 and OP-3, pushing up the road, towards the FRONT GATE.

Among them: JAKE – IOC of OP-2. Plus BRIAN, MIKEY, KELLY, BOB, A.J., AARON, PETE, MO, and BROCK.

They have fought their way from their position to here.

They look wired.

FIRING as they move, up at the rooftops and windows.

RICOCHETS from incoming fire can be heard.

Past the blood trails and burning phosphorus, body parts, and abandoned gear from OP-1.

They push into –

73 **EXT. HOUSE/DRIVEWAY – DAY**   73

– the DRIVEWAY.

As BRIAN, BROCK, and KELLY take position either side of the FRONT GATE, firing –

– JAKE moves up the driveway.

Seeing the blood trails leading up to the house.

He's talking into his comms.

> JAKE
> (into radio)
> *We're making entry into your OP.*

> ERIK
> (over radio)
> *Copy.*

JAKE starts shouting.

> JAKE
> (shouting)
> *Blue, blue, blue. We're making
> entry. Blue, blue, blue.*

> BROCK
> (shouting)
> Blue, blue, blue.

74   **INT. HOUSE/HALL - DAY**   74

- SGT LAERRUS - covering the door to the hall.

> BRIAN (O.S.)
> *Frogman, Frogman, coming in.*

SGT LAERRUS dips his rifle.

> LT MACDONALD
> They made it here.

CUT TO -

75   **INT. HOUSE/HALL - DAY**   75

- RAY, coming OUT of his dissociated state, at the sound of
the arrival of OP-2 and OP-3.

He looks around, momentarily confused.

He sees ERIK is no longer with him.

He then sees that ERIK is in the bedroom, with the IRAQI
family, sitting on the edge of the bed.

76   **INT. HOUSE/KITCHEN - DAY**   76

OP-2 and OP-3 start flooding into the HOUSE, rifles at low
port.

The sound of gunfire seems to be following them in.

They burst through -

- into the kitchen, then into -

75.

77 **INT. HOUSE/HALL - DAY** 77

- the hall.

There is the strange sense of collision, as the soldiers of
OP-1 watch their NAVY SEAL colleagues enter.

On the faces of RAY, TOMMY, SGT LAERRUS, LT MACDONALD - there
is huge relief.

On the faces of OP-2 there is shock, as they see wounds on
ELLIOTT and SAM. The blood - that has spread everywhere.
The horrific nature of the injuries.

BRIAN, a GUNNER in OP-2, is one of the first in.

BRIAN is older than the others. He's 32. A veteran of
Afghanistan, and on his second tour in Iraq.

He's also half-Iraqi. He has many family in Baghdad.

He's followed directly by the AOIC of OP-2 - JAKE.

TOMMY NOTICES - JAKE has hot phosphorus shrapnel, stuck to
one boot. Smoking.

RAY looks at BRIAN.

Sees his wide eyes, staring at ELLIOTT.

RAY raises his voice to speak to the room.

It sounds as if he's taking control of the moment. But
inside, he's handing control to the others.

>   RAY
>   All right, guys - check it out -
>   we've got multiple leg injuries
>   here. I need morphine. Gauze.
>   Give me whatever you've got. And
>   there's guys on the roof.

>   JAKE
>   Mikey. Brian. Go. Get up there.

OP-2 SEALS MIKEY and BRIAN head to the stairway.

As they do so, BRIAN and MIKEY glimpse ERIK in the downstairs
bedroom.

BRIAN is amazed momentarily by the sight of ERIK.

ERIK sitting on the bed. His helmet off. He looks dazed.
His head in his hands.

76.

The sight of ERIK also jolts MIKEY. It scares him. Somehow this is more alarming to him than the sight of the wounded.

He realises: *we could all die here today*.

Then they move up the stairwell to FRANK.

> RAY
> (to Jake)
> We need to get these guys the fuck out of here, *now*.

> JAKE
> Have you called for casevac?

> RAY
> I can't punch out from here.

JAKE turns to JOHN - OP-2 COMMS.

> JAKE
> (to John)
> Can you make comms?

> JOHN
> Yessir.

BRIAN starts handing all his medical kit to RAY.

As he does so, JAKE pushes past BRIAN -

- into the DOWNSTAIRS BEDROOM.

78 **INT. HOUSE/DOWNSTAIRS BEDROOM - DAY** 78

JAKE looks at ERIK.

Immediately assessing ERIK'S head-space. Immediately worried.

> JAKE
> Sir. Has anybody looked at you? Checked you out?

ERIK looks up at JAKE.

> ERIK
> Elliott and Sam are wounded.

> JAKE
> ... Yeah. Hey, man, take a knee. Let me do a blood sweep.

77.

ERIK kneels.

As JAKE talks, he is checking around ERIK'S for blood/injury.

                    JAKE (CONT'D)
          What calls have been made? Is the
          casevac platform coming back here?

ERIK looks JAKE in the eyes.

                    ERIK
          Dude, I'm fucked up. I need you to
          take point.

A beat between them.

JAKE'S recognition of ERIK'S state, and ERIK'S recognition of his own state.

ERIK handing over leadership at this moment is itself an act of leadership.

                    JAKE
          Roger that.

AT THAT MOMENT -

- the sound of GUNFIRE from upstairs starts.

79   **INT. HOUSE/HALL - DAY**   79

BRIAN heads towards the stairwell, following after MIKEY.

OP-2 are continuing to cram into the small hall area.

Another of the OP-2 SEALS - BROCK - enters the cramped hall, hooting and hollering.

He's amped up. But it feels weirdly performative. Misjudged.

                    BROCK
          Let's *GO*, boys. Let's fucking *DO*
          this.

BROCK nearly treads on ELLIOTT as he enters.

                    LT MACDONALD
          Whoa - dude - watch it.

But OP-2 continues to cram into the space.

Another guy accidentally kicks SAM - and SAM screams.

RAY stands.

>   RAY
>   HEY! I know we're moving fast but
>   don't step on anyone's fucking
>   legs!

BROCK doesn't seem to hear.

He looks down at SAM.

>   BROCK
>   All right, Sammy. Let's GO.

He's trying to fire SAM up.

But SAM is barely conscious through the morphine, pain, and blood loss.

SAM starts getting agitated.

>   RAY
>   (to Brock)
>   Hey - chill out.

BROCK again ignores, or doesn't hear. And gives SAM a 'buddy' tap on the leg -

>   BROCK
>   My man - let's do this!

- and SAM SCREAMS.

RAY palms BROCK in the chest. Hard.

Knocks him back.

>   RAY
>   Bro, get the *fuck* away.

BROCK stares at RAY.

CUT TO -

80   <u>**INT. HOUSE/UPSTAIRS MAIN ROOM - DAY**</u>   80

- BRIAN pushing through the metal door -

81   <u>**EXT. HOUSE/BALCONY-ROOF - DAY**</u>   81

For the first time, we see the ROOF/BALCONY AREA.

79.

As BRIAN exits –

– he sees a glimpse of an enemy fighter, on the roof of the building directly beside them.

BRIAN immediately opens fire.

He fires eight to ten rounds from his MARK 48. A large, heavy, belt-fed machine gun.

Then he ducks down –

– and becomes aware of incoming and outgoing fire from behind him.

He moves slightly along the wall.

Ducks up.

Fires another burst.

More incoming fire.

He crawls behind the low wall again to find a new position.

He sees MIKEY doing the same thing on the other side of the roof.

BRIAN is surging with adrenalin – but through it is coming an awareness. A sense of being surrounded, and overpowered.

CUT TO –

INT. HOUSE/HALL – DAY   82

– AARON, moving in and situates himself by Elliott.

>   AARON
>   Fill me in.

>   LT MACDONALD
>   He got hit in both legs. The
>   shoulder. And he's got wounds on
>   lower abdomen. Lost a lot of
>   blood.

>   AARON
>   Okay.

>   LT MACDONALD
>   There's something burning inside
>   him.

                    AARON
          That's phosphorus. It's all over
          outside.

AARON is checking the tourniquets on ELLIOTT'S legs.

                    AARON (CONT'D)
          Bro, great fucking job with the
          tourniquets.
                    (reassuring Elliott)
          Yeah - you're going to be all good,
          brother. All good. You just hang
          tight. We're going to get you the
          fuck out of here.

                    ELLIOTT
          Did you hit me with morphine?

                    LT MACDONALD
          You've had morphine.

                    AARON
          When?

                    LT MACDONALD
          Uh - like minutes ago. Just before
          you guys rolled in.

                    ELLIOTT
          Did you do it in my arm? Bad blood
          return in the legs. Got to be the
          arm.

                    LT MACDONALD
          It was your arm, bro.

                    ELLIOTT
          Got to be the arm.

                    LT MACDONALD
          It was.

                    ELLIOTT
          Morphine will wear off real quick.

                    AARON
          You're doing great, bro.

CUT TO -

- JAKE, re-entering the hall from the downstairs bedroom.

Inside, he has a massive sense of foreboding and urgency.

81.

But he speaks with clarity, efficiency, and control.

> JAKE
> Okay, guys. Listen up. Everybody.
> Start doing a reorg. We're going
> to get these guys casevaced.

JAKE turns to JOHN.

> JAKE (CONT'D)
> John, we're going to get four
> Bradleys over here. Two for our
> extraction, two for casevac. I
> want the casevacs either side of
> the front gate. Brad one will be
> right. Brad two will be left.

> JOHN
> Yessir.

JAKE'S manner is cutting through the haze of shock that has
permeated the house since the IED explosion.

ERIK emerges from the downstairs bedroom.

JOHN starts calling in.

> JOHN (CONT'D)
> (into radio)
> Manchu X-Ray, this is Frogman-5
> Romeo. We need a casevac from OP-
> 1 building, four Bradleys, two for
> casevac of two severely wounded.
> Break. Pick-up will be at front
> gate, to position either side.
> Over.

CUT TO -

- RAY and BROCK, with SAM.

> RAY
> I'll take his legs. You'll get his
> arms.

> SAM
> You going to move me?

> RAY
> Yeah. We are.

> SAM
> No - no - don't do that -

                    BROCK
          You're going to have to frogman up,
          bro.

                    SAM
          Don't fucking touch me! Don't
          fucking do it!

                    BROCK
          There's no choice, bro.

CUT TO -

- JOHN. Listening to his headphones.

Then says to JAKE.

                    JOHN
          They're waiting on brigade
          approval.

ANGER flashes on JAKE'S face.

                    JAKE
          What the *fuck*?

                    JOHN
          Because the last tanks got fucked
          up, sir. They won't send casevac
          unless the CO gives the thumbs-up.

                    JAKE
          Motherfuckers.

                    AARON
          We've got to get them out, sir.

                    JAKE
          On it.

JAKE stares at ELLIOTT for a beat.

Then looks back to JOHN.

                    JAKE (CONT'D)
          You've got to be the CO.

                    JOHN
          Sir. Say back.

                    JAKE
          Radio them right now. Say you're
          the CO. Give them the order to
          send the fucking tanks.

Beat.

JOHN absorbing what he's being told to do.

JOHN is twenty-one years old, in combat with overwhelming enemy forces, surrounded by blood and horrifically injured comrades - and he's being asked to impersonate a colonel.

Then -

>   JOHN
>   (totally calm)
>   Roger that.
>   (into radio)
>   Manchu X-Ray, this is Manchu-6.
>   You are authorised to push casevac
>   platforms into Frogman position.

Beat. Listening.

>   JOHN (CONT'D)
>   (calm)
>   Affirmative, Manchu X-Ray. You are
>   authorised.

JAKE watching.

Then JOHN turns to JAKE.

>   JOHN (CONT'D)
>   Bushmaster is approved to manoeuvre
>   to our position.

JAKE nods.

Addresses the room.

>   JAKE
>   (radios)
>   Mikey - Brian - give me an update
>   on the roof.

>   MIKEY
>   (over radio)
>   Holding security.

>   JAKE
>   Are we up on all gear?

>   A.J.
>   There's gear in the street.

>   JAKE
>   We'll get it. You're with me.

                    KELLY
          I'll roll with you guys.

CUT TO -

83   **EXT. ROAD - DAY**   83

- the ROAD.

The burning phosphorus patches.

The sound of the gunfight over the rooftops.

JAKE and A.J. emerge.

Gunfire is all around.

KELLY takes position by the gate.

As JAKE and A.J. recover the scattered kit -

- figures with AK-47s become visible on the rooftop opposite.

KELLY starts shooting at them.

One is obviously hit.

CUT TO -

84   **EXT. HOUSE/BALCONY-ROOF - DAY**   84

- BRIAN and MIKEY.

The incoming fire from the surrounding buildings is too
intense.

They start to back away, crawling as low as they can towards
the METAL DOOR.

BRIAN is last through, on his stomach.

Pushing his machine gun ahead of him.

85   **INT. HOUSE/HALL - DAY**   85

JAKE re-enters the HALL.

Sees -

- BOB, standing in the bedroom with ERIK.

BOB is the PLATOON CHIEF - senior in rank to SAM, lower than JAKE and ERIK.

He is supposed to be tactical expert.

He's doing nothing. He's just staring into space.

JAKE looks at BOB in disgust.

> JOHN
> Bradleys are four minutes out.

JAKE goes to the base of the stairwell.

Calls up.

> JAKE
> What's going on? Casevac is
> inbound. I need a 5W.

FRANK moves upstairs.

SEES - BRIAN and MIKEY holding security on the metal doorway, from the top of the stairs.

> BRIAN
> We had to suck back. Unable to
> hold position.

FRANK calls back.

> FRANK
> Multiple bad guys trying to get to
> our position.

JAKE turns back to the men crammed into the hallway.

> JAKE
> When the Bradleys get here, Aaron
> and Tommy - you grab Elliott. You
> guys are going to head out first.

TOMMY nods.

> JAKE (CONT'D)
> You're going to go into Brad one.
> Right-hand side.

> AARON
> Right-hand side. Check.

> JAKE
> Ray and Brock, grab Sam. Brad two.
> Left side.

                    RAY
          Got it.

                    JOHN
          Bradleys are three minutes out.

                    JAKE
          Let's get these guys ready to move.

RAY takes hold of the pants material around SAM'S legs.

SAM screams.

BROCK is at SAM'S shoulders.

TOMMY moves to ELLIOTT.

                    AARON
          Okay - let's sort this shit out.
          Get that rug!

BROCK grabs the rug from the room beside them and drags it
over.

                    AARON (CONT'D)
          Fold it. Yo, Tommy. With Mac.
          You guys roll him.

                    TOMMY
          Got it.

                    AARON
          Roll him on three. One, two,
          three.

ELLIOTT moans as TOMMY and LT MACDONALD roll him.

AARON and BROCK get the rug under him.

                    AARON (CONT'D)
          Okay. Set him down. On three.

                    ALL TOGETHER
          One, two, *three*.

They lay him flat, then pull him over to the other side to
get the rest of the rug out from underneath him.

ELLIOTT is now in place.

86   **<u>INT. HOUSE/UPSTAIRS MAIN ROOM - DAY</u>**   86

BRIAN is through the METAL DOOR.

He picks up his MARK 48, and backs away to the entrance to the stairwell.

Then turns.

Holds his sights on the metal door.

Totally focused. Unaware of anyone around him.

Purely fixated on shooting the first person who follows him through.

87   **INT. HOUSE/KITCHEN - DAY**   87

The four-man protection team position by the FRONT ENTRANCE, ready to move.

Outside - we hear the sound of the TANKS approaching.

CUT TO -

88   **INT. HOUSE/HALL - DAY**   88

- JOHN.

> JOHN
> Bradleys are two minutes out.

RAY looks for his purchase on SAM.

RAY speaks to SAM.

> RAY
> Hey man, this is it. It's going to
> hurt. Get ready.

> SAM
> No, no - there's got to be another
> way.

> RAY
> There's isn't.

> BROCK
> BTF up, bro.

> SAM
> (psyching himself up)
> Fuck, fuck, fuck -

BEHIND them, ELLIOTT moans in pain.

                    ERIK
          We're getting Elliott out on the
          right?

The sounds of the wounded are drowned out by a THIRD PASS
from the FIGHTER JET.

Again, everyone is deafened.

RAY watches ERIK and JAKE - pausing because of the noise.

He can see the expressions on their faces. The tension, and
adrenalin.

When the JET NOISE SUBSIDES -

                    JAKE
          Check. Elliott right side. Sam
          left side.

                    JOHN
          Bradleys are one minute out.

ERIK bumps TOMMY out from his position with ELLIOTT.

                    JAKE
          Frank. Kelly. You're going to
          break us out. Gunners, you'll set
          up security out on the street.

The sound of the TANK ENGINES penetrate the house.

RAY chooses his purchase on SAM'S leg - the material of his
pants, just below the knee.

SAM starts screaming again as RAY bunches the material in his
fist.

JAKE turns to the guys about to carry the wounded.

                    JAKE (CONT'D)
          You guys good? We're about to
          move.

JAKE gets 'checks' from the guys.

                    JOHN
          Bradleys are here.

                    JAKE
          Okay, we're moving.

                         ERIK
                    (lifting Elliott)
          One, two, three -

                         JOHN
                    (into radio)
          Ramp down, ramp down.

                         JAKE
                    (shouts)
          Breakout, breakout.

89   **EXT. HOUSE/COURTYARD - DAY**   89

The FOUR-MAN SECURITY TEAM, providing cover for the
extraction, push out of the FRONT ENTRANCE.

90   **INT. HOUSE/HALL**   90

Outside, the sound of GUNFIRE immediately starts up again.

                         JAKE
               Go, go, go.

AARON, ERIK, and LT MACDONALD, and PETE lift ELLIOTT and
start to move.

As they move, LT MACDONALD'S radio handset gets stuck on the
side of the door.

ERIK reaches to it. Rips it out - tearing out the wiring as
he does so.

                         SAM
               Oh fuck, oh fuck -

                         JAKE
               Ray, Brock - GO.

                         RAY
               Let's go.

RAY and BROCK lift SAM.

SAM cries out.

                         RAY (CONT'D)
                    (to Sam)
               Look at me, bro. The whole way.
               I got you.

And start carrying him out -

90.

91   **INT. HOUSE/KITCHEN - DAY**   91

- through the kitchen -

92   **EXT. HOUSE/COURTYARD - DAY**   92

- to the COURTYARD.

93   **EXT. HOUSE/DRIVEWAY - DAY**   93

As they enter the short driveway -

- TWO strange things are happening. Surreal in their
juxtaposition.

The FIRST is that they are being shot at.

Gunfire is coming in from the rooftops around them.

In particular, it is coming from the rooftop of the same
HOUSE they are leaving.

Enemy fighters have already occupied exactly the area where
BRIAN and MIKEY were fighting, only minutes ago.

We see the ATTACKERS briefly as they fire down. They are no
more than glimpsed shapes, and muzzle flashes.

The SECOND is that as he is carried, SAM'S pants are slipping
down. And as they slip, RAY has to grab more material.

Meaning that SAM is soon naked from his waist to his knees.

The lack of dignity, while being shot at, is a strange
combination. It's dissonant. If they're about to be killed,
it feels it shouldn't be this way.

This image - moment - sears itself on RAY'S mind.

CUT TO -

94   **INT. HOUSE/HALL - DAY**   94

DELETED

95   **INT. HOUSE/UPSTAIRS MAIN ROOM - DAY**   95

DELETED

91.

96   **EXT. ROAD - DAY**   96

- outside.

RAY, SAM, and BROCK.

They have reached the METAL GATE, and are exiting back into
the road -

- where the two BRADLEY TANKS are waiting, rear ramps down,
ready to take the wounded.

The gunfire is deafening.

AARON and TOMMY have already got ELLIOTT half-inside TANK
ONE.

Ahead of RAY - PETE - has already climbed into TANK TWO.

Maybe out of fear.

97   **INT. TANK TWO - DAY**   97

BROCK climbs up the ramp, into the back of TANK TWO, pulling
SAM with him.

RAY follows, holding SAM'S legs.

As they get him inside -

- BULLETS start hitting the outside of the BRADLEY.

Incredibly loud, as they slam into the metal. Incredibly
jarring.

RAY looks out the back of the TANK, and sees, through the
open ramp door -

- for the FIRST TIME since the attack started -

- a CLEAR VIEW of one of the attackers.

It's a young man.

He's running across the road, a hundred metres away, from
left to right.

Holding a weapon.

Crouched in the cramped space, RAY lifts his rifle, and
starts firing.

As he fires -

92.

- the RAMP of the TANK starts rising.

RAY realises they are about to be trapped in the Bradley.

He stops firing.

Shouts.

>   RAY
>   *No - no - Wait, wait, wait - I've*
>   *got to get out -*

But the door closes.

The TANK starts moving.

Not waiting.

Leaving.

RAY looks stunned.

CUT TO -

98   **EXT. ROAD - DAY**   98

- the soldiers outside, falling back to the house, as the
BRADLEYS start to move away.

ERIK is yelling at LT MACDONALD.

>   ERIK
>   GET BACK! GET BACK!

As LT MACDONALD runs -

- he slips on dust and dirt and blood on the leaf of the
metal gate, that was lying on the road.

He falls flat on his face.

As he scrambles up, he sees ERIK, holding position by the
gate.

They lock eyes.

>   ERIK (CONT'D)
>   Thought you were hit.

>   LT MACDONALD
>   I slipped.

Surprisingly, ERIK smiles.

A sudden, strange almost normal moment of contact in the chaos.

99   **INT. HOUSE/HALL - DAY**   99

As all remaining SEALS collapse back into the house -

- JAKE starts issuing orders.

JOHN relays radio communication to JAKE.

> JOHN
> ISR says people are moving to our
> rooftops. They're telling us to
> get our guys off right now.

> JAKE
> (yells upstairs)
> Clear the top deck!

CUT TO -

- MIKEY, hitting BRIAN on the shoulder.

> MIKEY
> *Move, move. Let's fucking move.*

BRIAN and MIKEY start backing down the STAIRWELL to the landing.

> JAKE
> Do we still have guys up there?

> MIKEY
> No way. We're the last guys.

> BRIAN
> They're right on us.

> JAKE
> Zawi - hold security there until I
> tell you to take it down.

JAKE shouts to the room.

> JAKE (CONT'D)
> (to everyone)
> LISTEN UP! I'm going to have the
> Bradleys take off the second floor
> of this building.

BRIAN looks stunned.

94.

For a moment - he can't compute.

JAKE is saying that the tanks are going to fire on the
building that they are all hiding inside.

>   JAKE (CONT'D)
>   Gunners, you're holding security on
>   the street for extract.

>   BRIAN
>   (to Mikey)
>   I got it. Go.

MIKEY heads to the kitchen for preparation for breakout.

>   JAKE
>   Mac - I want a show of force for
>   when that happens.

CUT TO -

100   **EXT. ROAD - DAY**   100

- BRADLEYS THREE and FOUR arriving in the street.

CUT TO -

101   **INT. HOUSE/KITCHEN - DAY**   101

- JAKE, shouting into his radio.

>   JAKE
>   (into radio)
>   *I'm going to need you to fire into*
>   *top deck of our building! We have*
>   *enemy on our building and all*
>   *surrounding buildings.*

>   BRADLEY GUNNER
>   (over radio)
>   Say again - fire into your
>   building?

>   JAKE
>   *Fire into our building. Top deck.*

>   BRADLEY GUNNER
>   (over radio)
>   Negative, Frogman - we can't do
>   that.

                              JAKE
                         (into radio)
                    The top deck is fucking clear!
                    Fire into it!

                              BRADLEY GUNNER
                         (over radio)
                    Roger that. Stand by.

                              JAKE
                         (to Brian)
                    Zawi - get the fuck down here.
                         (to room)
                    SUCK IN. FIND COVER.

                              BRADLEY GUNNER
                         (over radio)
                    Going hot.

BRIAN gets down to the bottom deck, takes a knee, and gets
his head down.

CUT TO -

102   **EXT. HOUSE/ROAD - DAY**   102

- SUDDENLY, SHOCKINGLY LOUD -

- the BRADLEY TANK GUNNER in tank one opens fire -

- directly on the HOUSE.

Repeatedly hitting the top floor.

The top section of the house starts erupting with concrete
dust from the impacts.

CUT TO -

103   **INT. HOUSE - DAY**   103

- all remaining soldiers of OP-1 and OP-2, hunching down as
the tank rounds slam into the floor above them.

MIKEY is under the kitchen table.

BRIAN is at the base of the stairwell.

JAKE and ERIK are in the bedroom with the family.

The vibrations of the impacts shudder through the entire
building.

Dust rolls through the lower floor.

CUT TO -

104   **INT. HOUSE/DOWNSTAIRS BEDROOM - DAY**   104

- the faces of the IRAQI family as the top floor of their house is destroyed.

CUT TO -

105   **EXT. ROAD - DAY**   105

- the BRADLEYS -

- as BOTH TANKS extend their sweep of fire to start shooting at ALL THE TOP FLOORS of the surrounding residential houses.

A stunning explosion of gunfire.

Simultaneously both discriminate and indiscriminate.

Sustained.

For thirty full unrelenting seconds.

Then -

- it stops.

CUT TO -

106   **INT. HOUSE/DOWNSTAIRS BEDROOM - DAY**   106

- ERIK, staring at the IRAQI FAMILY.

The MAN is screaming at ERIK in IRAQI.

The MOTHER is shouting in English. One word.

> MOTHER
> WHY? WHY? WHY?

> ERIK
> I'm sorry. I'm sorry.

> MOTHER

> WHY? WHY?

CUT TO -

107   **INT. HOUSE/HALL - DAY**   107

       - JAKE.

                          JAKE
                 Breakout, breakout.

108   **EXT. HOUSE/COURTYARD/DRIVEWAY - DAY**   108

       The soldiers pour out of the building.

       As they move, they are firing on all angles, all at once.

       Into windows.

       Into doors.

       At rooftops.

109   **EXT. ROAD - DAY**

       MIKEY is out in the road first.

       TOMMY not far behind.

       Then BRIAN and A.J.

       There is no cover on the street. No concealment.

       From the rooftops, they can see muzzle flashes.

       They can see rounds landing in street.

       The four gunners give cover to everyone else -

       - 'singing' with each other. Firing in five-to-ten-
       round bursts, which the next gunner takes over, so there is
       never a break in the firing.

       Their barrels start to glow RED HOT.

       The remaining soldiers follow the gunners out, and start
       cramming into the backs of the BRADLEYS.

       The small tanks are barely big enough to contain all of them.

       They jam themselves inside.

       Compressing.

       TOMMY runs out of ammunition before he joins the others in
       the Bradleys.

98.

One of the last men inside is BRIAN.

As the rear doors of BRADLEY FOUR RISE, he is firing out the back.

Shouting -

> BRIAN
> Get the fucking ramp up!

The very last man in is ERIK.

Then the ramps are closed.

And the BRADLEYS drive away.

A few seconds later -

- the street is empty.

And silent.

CUT TO -

110   **INT. HOUSE/HALL - DAY**   110

- the hall.

Concrete dust from the tank fire is still gently rolling down from the stairwell.

Blood is smeared all over the floor.

Through the doorway to the downstairs bedroom -

- the IRAQI FAMILY are looking out.

The two GIRLS and the MOTHER are howling.

CUT TO -

111   **INT. TANK TWO - DAY**   111

- RAY.

Inside BRADLEY TWO.

He's breathing hard.

Bullets are still hitting the outside of the tank.

But as the TANK travels -

99.

- the gaps grow between the bullet impacts.

Then -

- they simply stop.

There is only the noise of the ENGINE.

It's low light, in the interior.

Dust from the road pushes in.

Fills the air.

In the dim cabin light, blood seems to be everywhere.

Sticky, black, smeared, or bright red and wet.

The smell of arterial blood is overpowering.

BROCK starts gagging.

PETE suddenly throws up.

BROCK throws up on SAM.

SAM jokes. Dry.

> SAM
> Brock. You're not helping.

FIGHTING his NAUSEA -

- RAY tries to pull SAM'S pants back up.

He does as best he can.

Then he sits back down.

In this dark space -

- grinding engine noise, dust, blood, vomit, heat -

- ONE FULL MINUTE PASSES.

Then ABRUPTLY -

- CUT TO BLACK

112   **BLACK SCREEN**   112

In the blackness -

Several seconds of silence.

Then, a FLURRY of voices.

> RAY (O.S.)
> - his leg -

> MEDIC (O.S.)
> Easy -

> MEDIC (O.S.)
> *Whoa* - don't fucking - you tipped
> him -

> MEDIC (O.S.)
> Just -

Abrupt silence.

A few seconds.

Then -

- the sound of ELLIOTT moaning.

> MEDIC (O.S.)
> Shears -

> MEDIC (O.S.)
> Cut it - cut them - get the boots -

> DOCTOR (O.S.)
> - Did you give him morphine?

> RAY (O.S.)
> Yes -

> DOCTOR (O.S.)
> What time?

> RAY (O.S.)
> - I don't know.

> DOCTOR (O.S.)
> How much?

> RAY (O.S.)
> I don't know. Just - what was
> there, in the -

> DOCTOR (O.S.)
> *You* put the tourniquet on?

101.

> > RAY (O.S.)
> > Yes, I did -

> > DOCTOR (O.S.)
> > What time?

> > RAY (O.S.)
> > - I don't know.

Silence.

A few seconds.

Then -

- we are somewhere outside.

We can hear the sound of a CHINOOK HELICOPTEER.

> > SERGEANT (O.S.)
> > Yo - what do you need from me?

> > RAY
> > I need to get back out there - I
> > need Bradleys, I've got to get back
> > out -

Silence.

A few seconds.

Then -

- sudden blinding daylight.

As we **CUT TO** -

113   **<u>EXT. CORPS AREA SUPPORT HOSPITAL - DAY</u>**   113

- ELLIOTT being pushed out of a HOSPITAL TENT into bright
daylight.

He is on a wheeled stretcher, being pushed by ARMY MEDICS,
towards a CHINOOK.

His legs are bandaged.

He has multiple tubes and drips.

As he is pushed, ELLIOTT looks up, dazed. Pupils dilated.

He sees -

- he is being pushed past RAY.

RAY is silhouetted against the bright sky.

ELLIOTT half smiles.

> ELLIOTT
> (drugged up, spaced out)
> Hey bro - what's up -

> RAY
> I love you, man.

Then the stretcher has pulled RAY out of view.

RAY is gone.

Just the sky above ELLIOTT.

ON THIS -

- CUT TO RAY.

On his face.

Behind his eyes - dismay. Hope. Need.

END

CIVIL WAR

A Garland V.05

2.

OPEN ON -

INT. THE WHITE HOUSE - NIGHT

- a room in the White House.

Nondescript. A podium, and flags hanging behind.

The PRESIDENT enters.

He is white, white-haired, dark-suited. He has some of the approximate bearing of a statesman, but there's weird anger and intensity beneath.

He takes position at the podium.

Clears his throat.

He looks uncomfortable. Even nervous.

As he starts to speak, we realise he is rehearsing a presidential speech.

> THE PRESIDENT
> We are now closer than we have ever been -

He breaks off.

> THE PRESIDENT (CONT'D)
> We are now closer than we have ever been, to victory.

Beat.

> THE PRESIDENT (CONT'D)
> Some -

Beat.

> THE PRESIDENT (CONT'D)
> Some are already calling it the greatest -

Beat.

> THE PRESIDENT (CONT'D)
> Some are already calling it the greatest victory in the history of mankind.

Getting better.

3.

He starts to find his groove.

>   THE PRESIDENT (CONT'D)
>   We are closer than we have ever
>   been to victory. Some are already
>   calling it the greatest victory in
>   the history of military campaigns.

He smiles. Nods.

CUT TO -

INT. LIVE TELEVISISED BROADCAST - NIGHT

- the PRESIDENT making his live speech, straight to camera.

>   THE PRESIDENT
>   Today I can announce that the so-
>   called Western Forces of Texas and
>   California have suffered a very
>   great loss, a very great defeat, at
>   the hands of the fighting men and
>   women of the United States
>   military.

CUT TO -

INT. HOTEL BEDROOM - NIGHT

- a three-star hotel bedroom.

On the bed, we can see a press photographer's kit.

A helmet, a flak jacket, cameras, and lenses.

Outside the window, we can see the NEW YORK SKYLINE.

The PRESIDENT'S speech is playing on the TV.

As he speaks, a woman enters.

She's 40 years old. American.

The photographer.

>   THE PRESIDENT
>   The people of Texas and California
>   should know that they will be
>   welcomed back to these United
>   States as soon as their illegal
>   Secessionist government is deposed.

4.

LEE sits on the bed. Facing the TV.

She stares at the PRESIDENT.

Watching him.

> THE PRESIDENT (CONT'D)
> I can also confirm that the Florida
> Alliance has failed in its attempt
> to force the brave people of the
> Carolinas into joining the
> insurrection.

LEE picks up one of her cameras.

Zoom lens fitted.

She zooms in on the PRESIDENT'S face.

> THE PRESIDENT (CONT'D)
> Citizens of America, we are now
> closer than ever to a historic
> victory, as we eliminate the final
> pockets of resistance.

CLICK.

LEE takes the photo.

She lowers the camera, like a hunter, practising their kill-shot.

But continuing to gaze at the PRESIDENT.

> THE PRESIDENT (CONT'D)
> God bless you all. And God bless
> America.

AT THAT MOMENT -

- THROUGH THE HOTEL WINDOW, deeper in the city -

- a FIREBALL suddenly rises into the darkness.

A bomb, many blocks away.

A beat later, we hear the sound of the distant detonation.

As the hotel window shakes from the shockwave, LEE turns to look.

She watches blankly, as a secondary explosion sends a fireball into the air.

CUT TO -

EXT. NEW YORK - DAY

- NEW YORK CITY, seen from a distance.

In the foreground, smoke is rising from a burning building.

TITLE:

CIVIL WAR

EXT. BROOKLYN - DAY

AERIAL SHOT of a slightly battered 4X4 SUV car, driving through Brooklyn.

Painted white.

On the hood and sides, the word PRESS is written in large, black letters.

It passes a car park.

Instead of being full of cars, the car park is full of TENTS.

INT. CAR - DAY

Inside the car, LEE sits in the passenger seat.

Her colleague, JOEL, is driving.

Early forties, Latino, writer.

OUTSIDE THE WINDOW -

- we glimpse a squad of SOLDIERS on patrol.

They are in full combat gear - automatic rifles, helmets, flak jackets.

EXT. BROOKLYN - DAY

The car turns a corner -

- to their obvious destination.

6.

A little way ahead, the road is blocked by what looks like some kind of civil demonstration.

INT. CAR - DAY

JOEL pulls up to the sidewalk.

The moment the car stops -

- LEE immediately exits the vehicle. Carrying her camera.

JOEL reaches to the back seat of the car, where there is a pile of various stuff. Helmets, a ballistic vest, a gas mask.

He grabs a couple of fluorescent vests.

EXT. BROOKLYN/CROSS STREET - LATE AFTERNOON

The crowd are gathered around a cross street.

As LEE approaches, we see that most in the crowd are carrying water containers of one sort or another. Plastic canisters, water-cooler bottles, and buckets.

Parked in the centre of the cross street is a TRUCK with a large water container at the back.

This is not a demonstration.

These are desperate people, queuing for WATER.

RIOT POLICE surround the container, trying to manage a line to the back of the truck.

Some of the police hold automatic rifles. Some carry batons.

Nearby, a few journalists stand.

Most wear fluorescent vests, and have a gas mask strapped to a backpack. A few wear white helmets and flak jackets, with PRESS written in black marker.

Among them we see BOHAI - a Chinese photographer.

DAVE - a TV NEWS CAMERA OPERATOR.

DAVE spots LEE.

They nod at each other - familiar.

LEE scans.

7.

Sees tension. The anger in the crowd.

Sees the exhaustion in the cops. Behind their visors, they're dripping with sweat.

Then -

She notices another journalist.

Or - someone acting like a journalist.

A young woman.

This is JESSIE. She's twenty-three years old. She wears no protective gear, has two 35mm Nikon FE2 FILM CAMERAS slung around her neck, and a small backpack.

JESSIE has followed DAVE.

She's trying to get the same shot on her stills camera. But is more tentative. Hanging back slightly.

Only moving in when DAVE moves off.

But the moment DAVE captured has gone.

LEE watches the girl for a couple of moments.

Seeing her youth, and obvious inexperience.

The sight seems to transfix LEE for a moment. Displacing her from the surrounding chaos.

BEHIND LEE -

- JOEL has seen a journalist friend.

TONY. Chinese, late thirties.

The two men embrace warmly, pleased to see each other.

The relaxed good humour is dissonant with the sense of anger and chaos in the crowd.

> JOEL
> Lee.

LEE looks round.

Sees JOEL standing with TONY.

JOEL holds out the fluorescent vest for her to put on.

CUT TO -

8.

- in the crowd, the tension between the cops and the people
is suddenly starting to explode.

A fight breaks out.

CUT TO -

- two RIOT POLICE breaking ranks.

Moving forwards. Holding batons.

They reach into the crowd to grab a MAN.

It's unclear why.

The crowd around the man try to hold on to him, as the RIOT
POLICE try to drag him out.

A tug of war starts between the two cops and the crowd.

LEE lifts her camera and moves in.

Around her - other press photographers are doing the same.

But LEE moves differently to the others.

She steps almost *in* to the fighting.

As she shoots -

- we glimpse the young girl photographer.

JESSIE.

Though small, JESSIE has also put herself as close to the
action as she can.

But unlike LEE, it's too close.

A third COP breaks rank to assist his two colleagues -

- and swings with his baton. He's not particularly aiming
for JESSIE. He's just swinging for whoever is between him
and his colleagues.

But it strikes JESSIE on the side of the head.

She falls sideways.

Dazed.

LEE sees this.

She pushes herself forward out of the crowd.

9.

Gets a hand to JESSIE.

Grabs her arm.

Yanks her up.

Dragging her.

EXT. BROOKLYN/CROSS STREET - LATE AFTERNOON

LEE pushes the dazed girl away from the truck and the cops and the crowd.

As they walk:

> LEE
> You okay?

The girl nods.

> JESSIE
> I'm fine. I just - what happened?

> LEE
> You got hit.

LEE has reached JOEL'S car.

She turns JESSIE to lean against the hood, and looks into JESSIE'S eyes, checking concussion.

> JESSIE
> I got hit?

JESSIE suddenly frowns. As if just regaining focus.

And then is staring back at LEE. Wide-eyed.

> JESSIE (CONT'D)
> Oh fuck. No. *No* way.

> LEE
> What?

> JESSIE
> This is crazy. I don't believe it.
> You're Lee Smith. You're Lee
> fucking *Smith*.

A beat.

LEE'S face. Blank.

10.

Then she pulls off her fluorescent vest.

                    LEE
          Take this.

                    JESSIE
          Oh, no, I can't -

                    LEE
               (hard)
          Take it. Now. And put it on.

JESSIE does as she's told.

She looks suddenly like a kid who's been told off.
Embarrassed. Shamed.

LEE softens - very slightly.

                    LEE (CONT'D)
          You need to be more careful.

                    JESSIE
          ... I'm really sorry.

LEE looks back towards the water truck.

The commotion is continuing -

- and JOEL and TONY are walking back towards LEE and JESSIE.

Their backs to the truck.

JOEL and TONY saw what just went down with LEE and JESSIE.
JOEL looks half amused.

But behind them -

- something is happening.

A WOMAN has appeared.

She's come out of a side street.

And she's RUNNING FAST towards the TRUCK and the COPS and the
CROWD.

And as she runs - she's lifting something.

Holding it in the air.

It's a STARS AND STRIPES FLAG. Unfurling.

11.

In the commotion by the water truck, no one has seen what LEE can see.

CUT TO -

- LEE.

                    LEE
          Oh shit.

On instinct -

- LEE throws herself into JESSIE, knocking them both to the ground.

And half a beat later, the WOMAN has reached the crowd.

And a half-beat after that -

- she EXPLODES.

A massive suicide-bomb blast.

The crowd and the cops are engulfed.

CUT TO -

EXT. SKY - LATE AFTERNOON

- the sky.

Looking directly upwards.

Clouds catching light from a low sun.

CUT TO -

EXT. BROOKLYN/CROSS STREET - LATE AFTERNOON

- LEE, staring up at the sky.

Flat on her back.

Beats pass.

Then she sits up.

Gets to her feet.

She glances at JESSIE.

JESSIE seems uninjured.

Then LEE lifts her camera - and moves towards the hanging smoke.

CUT TO -

- JESSIE.

Picking herself up from the road.

Dazed.

She starts to walk away from the explosion.

Then -

- JESSIE stops.

And turns.

And faces the carnage behind her.

Hanging smoke. Multiple wounded. Multiple dead. Body parts in the road like bits of rubble.

The side of the truck is ripped open. Water has poured over the dead and wounded, creating a pool of bloody water.

And in the middle of the carnage -

- LEE is walking.

Taking photos.

JESSIE hesitates.

Then lifts her own camera -

- and photographs LEE.

CUT TO -

INT. HOTEL LOBBY - NIGHT

A hotel lobby.

INT. HOTEL BAR - NIGHT

At the hotel bar, there is an almost party vibe. Groups of journalists, talking and drinking.

The Chinese journalist TONY is sat at a table with BOHAI and a few other Asian press. They're raucous. Laughing.

13.

Near them a couple of TV camera teams are passing around and discussing a camera body. Their table is surrounded by Pelican cases.

One of them is DAVE.

Amidst this, on a table near the bar, WE FIND -

- LEE sitting with JOEL and SAMMY.

SAMMY is an African American journalist in his late sixties.

He has a walking stick resting on the chair. When he walks, it's with a limp.

LEE has a laptop open.

> LEE
> (mutters)
> Jesus the Wi-Fi is so fucking slow.

She's attempting to upload her pictures from earlier. Watching the blue bar crawl to 100%, in fits and starts.

JOEL and SAMMY are half drunk, and deep in journo conversation. Clearly, friends.

> JOEL
> The word I'm getting is July 4th.

SAMMY laughs.

> SAMMY
> The word you're getting. Like
> everyone in this room hasn't
> already heard this bullshit.

> JOEL
> July 4th, Sammy. The optics are
> irresistible. The Western Forces
> have stopped one hundred and twenty
> miles from DC. Texas and the
> Florida Alliance aren't far south
> of that.

> SAMMY
> The WF aren't stopped - they're
> stalled. They've lost their supply
> lines. But it's the race to
> Berlin. There's no coordination
> between the Secessionists. You
> watch: soon as DC falls, they'll
> turn on each other.

14.

JOEL laughs.

                         JOEL
           That's the most depressing thing I
           ever heard. What the fuck are you
           offering, Sammy? Eternal war?

                         SAMMY
           What are you expecting, Jo? The
           peace follows war is only ever
           peace for some. After Nuremberg -
           peace in Montana, sure. But not
           Korea, Vietnam, the Middle East.
           None of which were unconnected.

SAMMY lifts his beer.

                         SAMMY (CONT'D)
           And now there's no peace in Montana
           either.

                         LEE
           Huh. That's weird.

SAMMY and JOEL look round.

                         LEE (CONT'D)
           Jo was quoting himself earlier too.

JOEL glances at SAMMY.

                         JOEL
           Nailed?

                         SAMMY
           Yes.

JOEL and SAMMY both laugh.

                         LEE
           Writers. You're so needy.

                         JOEL
           Photographers care nothing for a
           turned phrase.

                         SAMMY
           But I do love you, Lee.

                         LEE
           I do love you too, Sammy.

AT THAT MOMENT -

15.

\- all the lights in the lobby go out.

LEE is only lit by the light from her laptop screen.

>   LEE (CONT'D)
>   Really?

>   SAMMY
>   It's every night this week.
>   They'll switch to the generator.

>   LEE
>   The upload was *this* close to done.

The lights flicker - then come back on.

LEE puts her laptop down.

>   JOEL
>   The eternal upload.

LEE reaches for her beer.

SAMMY watches her a moment. Seriousness now in his face.

Then he speaks. Casual tone. Very loaded.

>   SAMMY
>   So where you kids headed tomorrow?
>   Staying in New York a while, or
>   venturing out?

JOEL smiles.

>   JOEL
>   Fuck you.

>   SAMMY
>   Come on, Jo.

>   JOEL
>   So you can beat us there?

>   SAMMY
>   I couldn't beat you in a brisk
>   walk.

LEE takes a slug of her beer.

>   LEE
>   We're going to DC, Sammy. Tomorrow
>   morning. First thing.

SAMMY nods.

                    SAMMY
          Front line. I figured.

                    LEE   ·
          No. Not the front line. DC.

SAMMY, who was reclined in his seat, sits forward.

                    SAMMY
          ... What?

                    LEE
          I'm going to photograph the
          President. Jo's going to interview
          him.

SAMMY drops his voice.

                    SAMMY
          Photograph and interview the
          President. In DC.

                    JOEL
          That's the idea.

                    SAMMY
          What the fuck are you talking
          about? Are you serious?

SAMMY looks at LEE for confirmation.

She gazes back at him.

                    SAMMY (CONT'D)
          They shoot journalists in the
          capital on sight. They literally
          see us as enemy combatants.

                    JOEL
          Not a single interview in fourteen
          months.

                    SAMMY
          How are you going to do this?

                    LEE
          We get there. Before anyone else
          does.

                    SAMMY
          You think there's a rush to get
          executed on the South Lawn? You're
          in a race with *no one*.
                    (MORE)

                    SAMMY (CONT'D)
Okay - so you don't have a how.
Give me a *why*.

                    JOEL
Come on. We live for this.

                    SAMMY
Live for it? It will *kill* you.

                    JOEL
Sammy - July 4th, July 10th, West
Coast Forces or Portland Maoists -
it's all the same. DC is falling
and the President is dead inside a
month. Interviewing him is the
only story left.

                    SAMMY
Not a story if it never gets filed.
Lee - can I please talk you out of
this bullshit?

Throughout, LEE has been watching SAMMY closely.
Impassively.

She ignores his question.

                    LEE
What do you think the route's going
to be like?

A beat between them.

Then SAMMY exhales.

                    SAMMY
Driving?

                    JOEL
No, digging. We're going to tunnel
our way there.

                    SAMMY
There's nothing direct. The
Interstates are vaporised. And you
can't get anywhere near Philly, so
you've got to go west. Maybe as
far as Pittsburg. Then circle in
from West Virginia.

                    LEE
That's what we thought.

18.

                    SAMMY
          It's pretty wild out there, and
          only getting worse. The press
          credentials should keep you safe.

SAMMY pauses.

                    SAMMY (CONT'D)
          But when you get to DC, you should
          swap out the press pass for piano
          wire, so they can save bullets and
          string you up with it.

                    LEE
          You had that route already figured
          out, Sammy.

                    SAMMY
          ... Yeah. Okay.

Beat.

                    SAMMY (CONT'D)
          I'm kind of looking to get down
          there myself.

LEE and JOEL exchange a glance.

                    JOEL
          Knew it.

                    SAMMY
          Not DC. I don't want a piece of
          your suicide pact. I want
          Charlottesville. The front line.

SAMMY lifts a hand before they can speak.

                    SAMMY (CONT'D)
          Hear me out. Just because I'm a
          rival news outlet -

                    JOEL
          You're not a fucking rival, Sammy.
          We're Reuters, for Christ's sake.
          You think I care if you file with
          what's left of the *New York Times*?
          Win a Pulitzer, if there's any
          left. We'd be happy for you.

                    SAMMY
          You're worried I'm too old? Can't
          move quick enough?

19.

> LEE
> Aren't you?

> SAMMY
> Sure.   Yes.   But   -
>   (suddenly frustrated)
> You going to make me explain why I
> *have* to be there? Why I can't *not*
> be there?

LEE looks at SAMMY.

We see - affection.

> LEE
> No.

Beat.

> LEE (CONT'D)
> If it's the front line you want,
> half the press in here are going to
> be heading that way inside twenty-
> four hours.

> SAMMY
> You want me to walk around this
> fucking room, begging for a ride?

Silence.

Then LEE stands. Picks up her laptop.

> LEE
> I'm going to restart the upload in
> my room and crash out. Hopefully
> it will be done by the time I wake.

SAMMY is watching her.

She glances at him. Then back at JOEL.

> LEE (CONT'D)
> My vote. If Sammy wants to ride
> with us, I'm good with it. You two
> hash it out.

> SAMMY
> Thank you, Lee.

> JOEL
> Yeah, thanks. Make me the bad guy.

LEE starts walking away.

INT. HOTEL LOBBY/ELEVATORS - NIGHT

LEE walks to the elevators.

As she walks past the front desk -

> CONCIERGE
> Ma'am - just to warn you. If you
> take the elevator, we do sometimes
> have power cuts, which might mean a
> delay during your journey.

> LEE
> A delay?

> CONCIERGE
> We offer the option to use the
> stairs.

Beat.

> LEE
> I'm on the tenth floor.

> CONCIERGE
> Your choice, ma'am.

LEE continues walking to the elevators.

Then stops.

Looks at the elevators. Looks at the door to the stairs.

Sighs.

And is just opening the door to the stairs, when -

> JESSIE
> Ms Smith?

LEE turns.

And sees JESSIE standing behind her, holding the fluorescent
vest.

> JESSIE (CONT'D)
> Hey. It's me. Do you remember me?
> From earlier?

> LEE
> (thrown)
> ... Uh, yeah. How did you know I
> was staying here?

21.

                    JESSIE
              (cuts in, nervous)
         - I didn't mean to, like, stalk.
         But I know a lot of the press use
         this hotel. And - I wanted to say
         thanks. And I wanted to give you
         this back.

JESSIE holds out the vest.

                    LEE
         ... No. It's okay. Keep it.

                    JESSIE
         But -

                    LEE
         Keep it.

LEE turns to go.

Then stops herself. Looks back at the young woman.

                    LEE (CONT'D)
         And buy a helmet and some Kevlar,
         okay? If you're planning on
         attending any more stuff like that.

                    JESSIE
         I am planning on that. I'm a
         photographer. I want to be a war
         photographer, actually.

LEE gazes at the young woman.

She seems entirely guileless.

                    JESSIE (CONT'D)
         By the way, you've got the same
         first name as my hero. Lee Miller?
         She was one of the first
         photojournalists into Dachau. You
         know her stuff?

                    LEE
         ... Yeah. I know of Lee Miller.

                    JESSIE
         Of course.
              (hurried)
         But - I wanted to say that you're
         also one of my heroes. And you've
         got the same name too.

22.

LEE smiles.

> LEE
> Well, thanks. I'm in good company.

Beat.

> LEE (CONT'D)
> What's your name?

> JESSIE
> Jessie. Jessie Cullen.

> LEE
> So, Jessie, I've got to walk up ten flights of stairs. But - if I ever see you again, you'd better be wearing Kevlar and that fluorescent.

> JESSIE
> ... You bet.

LEE leaves into the stairwell door.

The door closes.

Leaving JESSIE alone.

A beat.

Then JESSIE turns.

She looks across the lobby, to the bar area.

The party vibe.

JOEL and SAMMY are still talking.

BOHAI is telling an animated story in Mandarin to his table.

TONY is laughing and contradicting.

A peal of laughter rolls towards JESSIE.

A beat.

Then JESSIE starts walking towards them.

CUT TO -

23.

INT. HOTEL ROOM/BATHROOM - NIGHT

- LEE.

She's lying in the bathtub.

But this isn't relaxation.

She feels very alone.

And she's frozen.

Covering her face in her hands.

CUT TO -

EXT. WAR - DAY/NIGHT

- a sequence of images of WAR.

Memories.

A street in Africa. A car reversing fast.

A street in the Middle East. A group of soldiers, running towards a burning building.

A cluster of palm trees - into which a rocket lands, and explodes.

Two men being beaten. Struck with a concrete block.

An execution, with a hand gun.

A dazed soldier, with a gaping head wound.

A patrol of soldiers, engulfed by an IED.

A man having a car tyre forced over his neck and shoulders, and set on fire.

And AMONG ALL THESE IMAGES OF WAR -

- LEE.

Photographing it all.

CUT TO -

INT. HOTEL LOBBY - NIGHT

- LEE.

24.

In the bath.

Dragging her hand away from her face.

Breathing out.

Processing.

Or trying to.

CUT TO -

EXT. NEW YORK - DAWN

- DAYBREAK.

A sequence of shots around NEW YORK.

6th AVENUE - blocked by a single TANK.

TENTS - laid out on the roof of a building.

GRAFFITI - 'Fuck the WF'.

A military SNIPER and SPOTTER - zeroing sights over the skyline.

CUT TO -

EXT. HOTEL ENTRANCE - EARLY MORNING

- LEE exiting the hotel.

She has her canvas camera bag and her rolling luggage.

Parked outside, she can see JOEL, standing by their PRESS SUV.

And there are silhouette figures on the back seats.

LEE frowns slightly as she approaches.

As she gets closer, on the back seat she sees SAMMY.

And then, sat beside SAMMY, JESSIE.

JESSIE sees LEE.

Waves. Holds up the fluorescent jacket.

LEE doesn't wave back.

25.

Instead, she walks straight up to JOEL.

> LEE
> A word.

EXT. HOTEL FORECOURT - DAY

LEE and JOEL move a little distance from the car.

> LEE
> What the fuck is that girl doing
> here?

> JOEL
> Right, so - she came over to the
> table last night after you went to
> bed. We got talking, and - she's
> very cool. Wanted to tag along.

> LEE
> So she's coming with us.

> JOEL
> What? You let *Sammy* tag along.
> You think he's going to do well,
> running for cover? Rounds flying
> over his head?

> LEE
> She's a *kid*. Did you notice that?

> JOEL
> Lee, she's like twenty-three, and
> she wants to do what we do. What
> *you* do. And - we all had to start
> one day. Were you much older than
> she is now?

LEE looks over at the car.

Sees JESSIE looking back at her. Nervously.

LEE looks back at JOEL.

Not happy.

> LEE
> Whatever happens, she goes no
> further than Charlottesville.

LEE starts walking back towards the car.

26.

EXT. FREEWAY - DAY

The car drives down a freeway.

JOEL is driving.

LEE sits in the front seat. She looks pissed off.

SAMMY and JESSIE in the back.

The road is almost empty. The only cars travel in the
opposite direction.

Reveal -

- ahead, the freeway is blocked by a massive jam of rusted
and burned-out vehicles. It's the road to Basra.

JOEL peels off at the next exit.

EXT. CHECKPOINT - DAY

A smaller road.

We watch from a distance.

The car is pulled up at a military checkpoint.

JOEL is out of the car. Talking to AMERICAN SOLDIERS.

Talking. A little laughing.

Then JOEL gets back into the car, and they are waved through.

INT. CAR - DAY

Inside the car, JOEL and SAMMY are trading JOEL'S prospective
interview questions.

JESSIE is listening. So happy to be where she is right now.

>   SAMMY
>   'Mr President, do you regret any
>   actions implemented during your
>   third term of office?'
>
>   JOEL
>   I'm not going to softball him,
>   Sammy.

                    SAMMY
          'In retrospect, Mr President, do
          you still think it was wise to
          disband the FBI?'

                    JOEL
          Passive-aggressive.

                    SAMMY
          'Sir, how is your policy evolving
          on the use of air strikes against
          American civilians?'

JOEL laughs.

                    JOEL
          Now you're talking.

                    SAMMY
          Just get the words out before the
          piano wire gets too tight.

LEE spots something in the road ahead.

                    LEE
          There's a gas station up ahead. It
          looks open.

                    JOEL
          We've got over half a tank. What
          do you think?

                    SAMMY
          Any chance to refuel, we should
          take.

                    JOEL
          Okay.

<u>EXT. GAS STATION - DAY</u>

JOEL pulls in to the gas station.

He stops one of the pumps.

There are three men sat over the entrance to what was once
the gas station store. All with automatic rifles.

By the pumps, there's another, armed.

When JOEL turns off the engine, the man by the pumps walks
over. Not exactly threatening. But not friendly.

28.

JOEL and LEE get out as he approaches.

>   GAS STATION GUARD 1
>   Help you, folks?

>   JOEL
>   We're just looking for gas.

>   GAS STATION GUARD 1
>   Got a local fuel permit?

>   JOEL
>   No. We're passing through.

>   GAS STATION GUARD 1
>   Can't help. Sorry.

The guard turns away.

>   LEE
>   Sir.

The man looks back.

>   LEE (CONT'D)
>   If we pay.

>   GAS STATION GUARD 1
>   I was never going to give it for
>   free.

>   LEE
>   I mean pay over the odds.

>   GAS STATION GUARD 1
>   What's over the odds?

>   LEE
>   Three hundred dollars. We need
>   half a tank, and two of your
>   canisters.

The man laughs.

>   GAS STATION GUARD 1
>   Three hundred dollars buys you a
>   sandwich. We got ham or cheese.

>   LEE
>   Three hundred Canadian.

The guard hesitates.

Then looks over to his colleague. And nods.

                                                           29.

                    GAS STATION GUARD 1
          Okay.

As LEE starts to hand over the cash -

- CLICK. JESSIE's door opens, and she gets out.

JOEL sees.

                    JOEL
          Stretching your legs?

                    JESSIE
          No - I saw something from the road.

                    JOEL
          ... This isn't going to take long.

He's trying to imply she should get back in the car.

She doesn't seem to realise.

                    JESSIE
          Sure.

JESSIE keeps walking.

LEE watches her go.

Then notices an exchanged glance between three armed men by
the store entrance.

One of them detaches and follows JESSIE.

LEE looks back at the GAS STATION GUARD 1.

Her gaze suddenly level, and hard.

                    LEE
          Are we good?

                    GAS STATION GUARD 1
          Yeah, don't worry. We're good.

LEE hesitates a moment.

Then follows JESSIE.

EXT. CAR WASH - DAY

LEE walks around the back of the gas station - where there is
a CAR WASH.

30.

Long unused now.

And hanging inside car wash, by their arms, are two men.

CAPTIVES. Stripped to their waist. Bruised. Battered.
Streaked in blood. Some fresh; some black, and crusted.

JESSIE stands a few metres away.

Pale, frozen by the sight.

The cameras hanging loose by her sides.

Just behind her is the armed GUARD that followed her.

LEE walks over to where JESSIE and the GUARD stand.

When the GUARD speaks, he feels wired. Drunk, or high.

> GAS STATION GUARD 2
> I told her. I don't mind her
> looking.

> LEE
> ... Who are they?

> GAS STATION GUARD 2
> Looters.

One of the CAPTIVES, barely conscious, murmurs:

> CAPTIVE
> I got kids.

> GAS STATION GUARD 2
> I actually know that guy. We were
> in high school together. Never
> talked to me much. More talkative
> now.

Beat.

> GAS STATION GUARD 2 (CONT'D)
> We've been debating what to do for
> two days now. Going round in
> circles.

The GUARD suddenly looks at JESSIE.

And smiles. Shows teeth.

> GAS STATION GUARD 2 (CONT'D)
> Tell you what. Why don't you put
> us and them out of our misery.
> **(MORE)**

31.

                    GAS STATION GUARD 2 (CONT'D)
          Make the call. I'll put rounds in
          them right now. Or we'll beat them
          up a little more, and chain them to
          the front. Cut 'em loose after a
          few days.

JESSIE is frozen.

                        GAS STATION GUARD 2 (CONT'D)
          Flip a coin if you like.

LEE acts.

She lifts her camera.

                        LEE
          Would you mind standing with them a
          moment?

                    GAS STATION GUARD 2
          Standing with them?

                        LEE
          Yeah. I'd like to take your
          picture.

Beat.

It feels long.

Then -

                    GAS STATION GUARD 2
          ... Okay. Just stand over there?

                        LEE
          Yeah.

He walks to the captives.

Turns.

                    GAS STATION GUARD 2
          Where do you want me?

                        LEE
          Maybe in between the two?

                    GAS STATION GUARD 2
          Gotcha.

CUT TO -

SILENCE THROUGH THE LENS.

The GUARD stands between the two men, holding his rifle.

Two branches of the tree spreading out above him like wings.

The two bloodied CAPTIVES hang either side.

CUT TO -

EXT. ROAD - DAY

- the SUV, driving fast.

Strapped to the back are two gas canisters.

INT. CAR - DAY

JESSIE is shaking.

> JESSIE
> I didn't take a photo. I didn't
> take a single photo.

No one says anything.

> JESSIE (CONT'D)
> I didn't even remember I had
> cameras. Like I didn't even -

JESSIE'S panic is growing.

> JESSIE (CONT'D)
> - Oh God. Oh my *God*. Why didn't I
> just tell him not to shoot them?

JOEL cuts in.

> JOEL
> Jessie - they're probably going to
> kill them anyway.

> JESSIE
> (agitated)
> How do you know?

> LEE
> He doesn't know. But it's beside
> the point. Once you start asking
> yourself those questions, and you
> can't stop. So we don't ask. We
> record - so other people ask. You
> want to be a journalist? That's
> the job.

33.

SAMMY glances at JESSIE. Sees the way she's shaking.

> SAMMY
> Hey. Lee.

> LEE
> What?

> SAMMY
> Back off.

> LEE
>
> What am I saying that's wrong?

> SAMMY
> I'm not saying it's wrong. She's
> just shook up.

> JOEL
> Lee doesn't understand shook up.

> LEE
> Whoa. *I'm* not being protective of
> her? Jo - you're the idiot who let
> her in this car. What happened
> back there is *nothing* in comparison
> to what we're heading into.

LEE turns around to face JESSIE in the rear seat.

> LEE (CONT'D)
> You need to understand where we're
> going is not -

LEE breaks off when she sees JESSIE'S face.

And turns back around.

> LEE (CONT'D)
> Holy shit. She's crying. The back
> seat is both a kindergarten and an
> old people's home. How did this
> happen?

> JOEL
> Lee! What the fuck.

> JESSIE
> (cuts in)
> Lee's right.

JESSIE is forcing control into herself.

                           JESSIE (CONT'D)
                    I won't make that mistake again.

Silence.

LEE glances back at JESSIE.

As if feeling a sudden moment of remorse. That she maybe she
went too far.

JESSIE is staring out of the window.

LEE looks back.

EXT. STRIP MALL - DAY

The car is driving past a STRIP MALL.

It's deserted, and was clearly the location of a fierce
battle.

The buildings are shot to bits.

Burned-out vehicles - military and civilian - litter the
parking lot.

As do corpses.

STRAY DOGS move through the wrecked area.

                         THE PRESIDENT (O.S.)
                    The terms of the so-called peace
                    summit could only be rejected,
                    fully rejected, by *all* right-
                    thinking Americans.

INT. CAR - DAY

The car is listening to THE PRESIDENT on the radio.

The signal is patchy. Distorted.

                         THE PRESIDENT
                    To the Secessionists, I say only
                    this: I pledge allegiance to the
                    flag of the United States of
                    America. We stand ready to fulfil
                    the promise of our forefathers. To
                    the flag, to the nation, and to
                    God.

LEE is still stewing.

35.

Then - as the car rolls past an intersection - she sees something in the adjacent street.

A crashed APACHE HELICOPTER. On its side, in the middle of the car park of a roadside strip mall.

LEE's gaze flicks to JESSIE, in the rear-view mirror.

Then to JOEL.

She lowers the volume on the radio.

>   LEE
> Stop here a minute.

>   JOEL
> This feel like a good place for a
> toilet break?

>   LEE
> Pull in.

JOEL stops the car.

LEE turns to JESSIE.

>   LEE (CONT'D)
> Come with me.

JESSIE looks nervous.

>   LEE (CONT'D)
> Just -

Beat.

>   LEE (CONT'D)
> Come with me.

EXT. STRIP MALL - DAY

LEE and JESSIE walk to stand in front of the downed Apache.

It's been sat here for some time.

It's listing to one side - obviously landed hard. Riddled with bullet holes. There are impact strikes all over the front glass, though the glass is still unbroken. All its blades except one are shattered.

The sun is behind it.

                    LEE
          Shoot it.

                    JESSIE
          ... Shoot the helicopter?

                    LEE
          Yeah. It's going to make a good
          image.

                    JESSIE
          ... Okay.

JESSIE lifts one of her cameras.

Starts shooting frames.

                    LEE
          FE2s. Don't see them around much.

                    JESSIE
          They were my dad's cameras
          actually.

LEE looks at her.

                    JESSIE (CONT'D)
          Don't worry. He's not dead. He's
          sitting in his farm in Missouri,
          pretending none of this is
          happening.

LEE nods.

JESSIE lowers her camera.

                    JESSIE (CONT'D)
          Lee -

Beat.

                    JESSIE (CONT'D)
          I'm sorry I jammed my way into your
          ride, okay? I know you're really
          angry about it. And I know you
          think I don't know shit. But -

                    LEE
          - I'm not angry about that, Jessie.
          I don't care what you do or don't
          know.

                    JESSIE
          Okay - but you are angry with me.

37.

LEE exhales.

JESSIE waits.

> LEE
> There is no version of this that
> isn't a mistake. I know because
> I'm it. Jo and Sammy are it.

Beat.

> JESSIE
> It's my choice.

LEE sighs.

> LEE
> Right. And I'll remember that,
> when you lose your shit, or get
> blown up, or shot.

JESSIE nods.

Looks away from LEE.

Then back.

> JESSIE
> Would you photograph that moment?
> If I got shot.

> LEE
> What do you think?

Silence.

CUT TO -

EXT. RAIL YARD - NIGHT

- a star-filled night.

The car is parked up in a rail yard, off the road.

Three-quarters of a mile away, where the tracks curve into
the distance, a battle is being fought.

There are alternating crackles of automatic rifle fire, and
thumps of something heavier.

Tracer rounds are clearly visible.

They arc as they fly.

38.

Sometimes they ricochet off whatever it is they are hitting, and spear crazily into the sky.

The sound of gunfire delays after each burst of streaking light.

Not much else can be seen.

A little distance from the car, LEE and SAMMY are sat on an abandoned sofa, watching the distant firefight.

> LEE
> Every time I survived a war zone, and got the photo, I thought I was sending a warning home. Don't do this. But here we are.

> SAMMY
> So it's existential.

> LEE
> What is?

> SAMMY
> What's eating you.

Beat.

> LEE
> Don't worry about me, Sammy.

Another stream of tracer fire. Then the delayed ripple of noise.

> SAMMY
> Am I allowed to say that I remember you at her age?

> LEE
> (anticipating)
> And I wasn't so different.

> SAMMY
> You weren't so different.

SAMMY glances at LEE.

> SAMMY (CONT'D)
> You think you're being hard on her. And I think you're being hard on yourself.

> LEE
> Okay, writer.

                    SAMMY
          God damn it, Lee. Stop. I'm
          speaking truth. And for the
          record, sure, I do worry about that
          girl. And I worry about you too.

                    JOEL
          What are you worrying about Lee
          for?

SAMMY looks round.

JOEL is approaching.

He has a bottle of vodka and is smoking a joint.

                    SAMMY
          ... Lee's lost her faith in the
          power of journalism. The state of
          the nation is QED.

                    JOEL
          Oh. Well I can't answer to that.

JOEL takes a drag on the joint.

                    JOEL (CONT'D)
          But I can tell you this gunfire is
          getting me extremely hard. Look at
          that shit light up the sky.

                    LEE
          It's not our story.

                    JOEL
          Yeah. But... you know. Bang bang.

JOEL takes a drag of the joint.

                    LEE·
          We're not going anywhere near there
          in the dark.

                    JOEL
          But sun-up.

Beat.

                    LEE
          Sun-up, if they're still at it,
          we'll take a look.

JOEL smiles.

                          JOEL
              Cool.

He hands the joint to LEE.

Then heads back to the car.

SAMMY and LEE sit in silence.

EXT. ROAD SIDE/CAR - NIGHT

At the back of the car, JOEL pulls out a sleeping bag and a
sleeping pad.

Then starts to lay it out alongside the vehicle.

JESSIE is sitting on the front passenger seat. She watches
JOEL prepare his bedding.

He notices her watching. Winks at her.

                          JOEL
              Action tomorrow.

                          JESSIE
              ... We're going down there?

                          JOEL
              Oh yeah.

JESSIE catches her breath. Involuntary. Hit by a sudden
rush of adrenalin.

                          JOEL (CONT'D)
              Not you. You're going to hang
              back.

                          JESSIE
              I don't want to hang back.

JOEL laughs.

                          JESSIE (CONT'D)
                  (firm)
              I don't want to hang back.

JOEL smiles.

                          JOEL
              You should see your face. Stomach
              doing turns, right? You won't get
              a minute's sleep tonight. My
              advice: don't expect to sleep.
                        (MORE)

41.

                    JOEL (CONT'D)
          That way, if you do, it's a nice
          surprise.

                    JESSIE
          ... Are you going to be able to
          sleep?

                    JOEL
          I've got out-of-date Ativan. Can
          give you some, if you like. Got
          plenty.

                    JESSIE
          No, it's okay.

                    JOEL
          ... Or I can stay up with you.
          Keep you company.

                    JESSIE
          No, I don't want to be - a burden.
          Or whatever.

                    JOEL
          Sure.

JOEL has finished laying out his bedding.

                    JOEL (CONT'D)
          But seriously, if you do get
          freaked out, wake me up. It's not
          nice being scared alone.

JESSIE smiles. Sincere. Grateful.

                    JESSIE
          Thanks, Jo.

JOEL smiles back.

CUT BACK -

- to LEE.

Now alone on the sofa.

Still watching the tracer fire.

CUT TO -

<u>**EXT. COMMERCIAL AREA - DAY**</u>

- a MILITIA SOLDIER.

42.

He's crouched behind the pillar of a low building, in the gap between two nondescript office buildings.

The pillar is large enough to give him cover - but only just.

He cowers as rounds hit the pillar and the wall behind him.

                    SOLDIER
          I can't - I can't fucking move -
          I'm going to get fucking hit -

The noise of the gunfire and impacts is extremely loud. Extremely jarring.

The SOLDIER starts screaming in alarm.

A few metres away, more MILITIA soldiers are stacked up by the corner of the building.

CROUCHED NEAR THEM -

- we find LEE, JOEL, and JESSIE.

LEE is crouched. Photographing.

She's wearing a white helmet and a blue ballistic vest. The vest has PRESS written in prominent white letters.

Behind her, flat against the wall, further away from the corner -

- JOEL and JESSIE. Also in helmets and vests.

JOEL'S expression is strange. His eyes are wide and wild. There's a rictus on his jaw. It almost looks like he's smiling.

JESSIE is trying to move forward. Trying to edge closer to LEE.

ONE OF THE MILITIA -

- a CORPORAL, yells at the SOLDIER under fire.

                    CORPORAL
          Stay small, Mike! Don't fucking
          move! We're going to pop smoke!
          Don't move!

The CORPORAL FIRES around the corner, at position from which MIKE is pinned -

- then turns to the men behind him.

43.

> CORPORAL (CONT'D)
> Jay - prep a smoke, get ready to
> move. Joe - take a fireteam and
> flank.

SOLDIER JOE looks back at him blankly. Frozen by the noise
and chaos.

The CORPORAL reaches out and grabs JOE by the shoulder strap
of his backpack. Speaks to penetrate his confusion.

> CORPORAL (CONT'D)
> Go *around* the building and *lay a*
> *base of fire.*

SOLDIER JOE moves off, followed by two of the squad.

AROUND THE CORNER -

- SOLDIER MIKE screams out as his backpack is hit, spinning
him around.

> CORPORAL (CONT'D)
> Are you hit? Mike?

SOLDIER MIKE keeps screaming.

The CORPORAL fires again around the corner.

When he pulls back, SOLDIER JAY has the SMOKE GRENADE ready
to throw.

> CORPORAL (CONT'D)
> Do it.

SOLDIER JAY tosses the SMOKE GRENADE.

The CORPORAL puts a hand on SOLDIER JAY'S back.

Thick white smoke starts floating past their position.

As the smoke starts to push out -

- the CORPORAL pushes SOLDIER JAY.

> CORPORAL (CONT'D)
> GO.

SOLDIER JAY moves to out of cover to the nearest pillar, and
starts putting down covering fire.

> CORPORAL (CONT'D)
> COME TO ME, MIKE! FUCKING MOVE!
> NOW - NOW - NOW -

44.

MIKE moves.

CUT TO -

- THROUGH LEE'S LENS.

As SOLDIER MIKE starts sprinting.

On the right of the frame, the CORPORAL and SOLDIER W are huddled up against the corner of the building.

Smoke drifting past them.

SOLDIER MIKE trying to cover the short distance to safety.

Then a round hits his pack.

It makes him trip.

He falls forward onto his hands and knees.

He looks up - seeming to look straight down the lens of LEE'S camera.

This moment is captured.

CUT TO -

- SOLDIER MIKE getting hit.

He's only a metre from the corner of the building.

But suddenly he just drops.

There's no spray of blood, or impact jerk. He just loses all motor power and flops face-down.

>   CORPORAL (CONT'D)
>   Mike's hit! I'm grabbing him - you
>   got me -

The SOLDIER JAY keeps firing.

As the CORPORAL moves around the corner to grab SOLDIER MIKE -

- SOLDIER W takes the CORPORAL'S position on the corner.

The CORPORAL grabs SOLDIER MIKE'S arm -

- and drags him the last metre, behind the cover of the corner.

                                                                    45.

                         CORPORAL (CONT'D)
                  Collapse, collapse - bump to me -

SOLDIER JAY moves back to cover, firing as he moves, and
bumps SOLDIER W off the corner position.

SOLDIER JAY swaps with SOLDIER W - JAY is moving while
firing, bumps W out of the way -

- as the CORPORAL pulls MIKE onto his back, and opens his
flak jacket.

As he does so, blood jets upwards from a wound in MIKE'S
torso.

The CORPORAL is yelling - some soldiers behind are frozen -
and MIKE is bleeding out.

                         CORPORAL (CONT'D)
                  He's got an abdominal - there's an
                  exit wound - I need a compression
                  bandage - apply pressure here -

LEE lowers her camera.

Sees JESSIE.

Crouched near the small group attempting to save SOLDIER
MIKE.

Photographing.

                         CORPORAL (CONT'D)
                  He's fucking gone -

CUT TO -

INT. OFFICE BUILDING/STAIRWELL - DAY

- sudden quiet.

Four MILITIA SOLDIERS, including the CORPORAL, still smeared
in MIKE'S blood, are moving up the stairwell of the office
building.

From deeper in the building, a high whimpering noise can be
heard.

Someone inside is wounded.

At the bottom of the stairwell, more SOLDIERS wait.

The three journalists are among them.

46.

Nobody talks.

The first four SOLDIERS all have their guns raised. Covering the stairwell ahead and above.

They have reached the top landing.

There's a doorway ahead. No door on the hinges.

CUT TO -

- LEE, edging forwards, up the first couple of stairs.

A SOLDIER catches her arm.

She looks round.

He shakes his head. Mouths: No.

CUT TO -

The CORPORAL holds out a hand, motioning.

One of the SOLDIERS hands him a grenade. The other SOLDIERS cover the landing.

The CORPORAL preps the grenade, then carefully tosses it through the doorway.

Underarm.

The grenade bounces into the room.

There's the sound of it hitting something. Furniture maybe. An office desk.

There's a pause, as all the SOLDIERS pull back slightly.

Two seconds. Feels like a long time.

Then a sudden detonation.

It makes everybody instinctively hunch.

In that moment -

- LEE again starts edging up the stairs.

This time, no one stops her.

ON THE LANDING -

- through the doorway, the grenade has set fire to something inside the office. There's flame somewhere. There's smoke.

47.

The SOLDIERS on the landing do nothing.

Just wait.

Strange beats pass.

The noise from inside. The SOLDIERS waiting in silence. Guns still trained on the doorway. LEE edging closer.

CUT TO -

SILENCE THROUGH THE LENS.

Now halfway up the stairs, looking up at the CORPORAL and the SOLDIERS on the landing.

This is captured.

CUT TO -

- the CORPORAL and his men moving into the room where the grenade was thrown.

LEE follows.

Inside, we see a WOUNDED SOLDIER propped against the back wall, with a long smear of blood where he has dragged himself along the floor.

As the MILITIA SOLDIERS enter, the WOUNDED SOLDIER lifts a hand -

- then is shot.

EXT. COMMERCIAL AREA - DAY

The office building is on fire.

Thick black smoke pours into the sky.

On road outside, JOEL and SAMMY are interviewing the CORPORAL. JOEL uses a digital recording device. SAMMY writes in a notepad.

Sat where the firefight took place, there are two HOODED PRISONERS.

JESSIE stands by the pillar where SOLDIER MIKE was shot: the area that was once entirely dangerous, and now is safe.

A few feet away, SOLDIER MIKE'S body lies under tarpaulin. One hand protruding, curled into a claw.

48.

LEE stands alone in the middle of the road.

Holding her helmet in one hand.

Staring at the burning building.

>   JOEL (O.S.)
>   *WOOOOOO!*

CUT TO -

INT. CAR - DAY

JOEL is driving fast. And he's totally wired.

>   JOEL
>   Holy fucking SHIT! Yes, yes, *YES!*
>   What a fucking RUSH!

EXT. REFUGEE CAMP - LATE AFTERNOON

The car is rolling into a refugee camp.

Lines of tents on the pitch of a football stadium. A sea of
them.

Children play in the gaps between.

The ground is dirt and mud.

The road is half-sunken wooden slats.

INT. CAR - LATE AFTERNOON

JOEL slows as he sees a couple of SOLDIERS up ahead.

They flag him down.

The SOLDIER leans down. Scopes out the occupants of the
vehicle.

>   SOLDIER
>   You're press? All of you?

>   JOEL
>   Yes, ma'am.

>   SOLDIER
>   IDs?

JOEL pulls a pass from a necklace inside his shirt.

49.

LEE and SAMMY do the same.

>   SOLDIER (CONT'D)
>   Okay. You staying the night?

>   JOEL
>   Just one.

The SOLDIER nods.

>   SOLDIER
>   Park where you can. There's a
>   canteen where you can eat. No
>   tents available.

>   JOEL
>   Thank you, ma'am.

EXT. REFUGEE CAMP/CANTEEN - SUNSET

JOEL and SAMMY sit outside an open canteen tent, eating off
paper plates.

In the stadium stands above them, a gang of kids play tag.

EXT. REFUGEE CAMP - SUNSET

In the stands on the opposite side of the stadium, JESSIE is
seated.

Hanging off the handrail beside her, a developed roll of
negatives is drying.

In her hands, she holds a compact Paterson developer tank -
about the size of a coffee thermos.

LEE approaches, carrying food on a paper plate. Rice, and
some kind of meat and vegetables in gravy.

>   LEE
>   Brought you something.

>   JESSIE
>   Thanks.

>   LEE
>   Don't forget to eat.

>   JESSIE
>   I'm starving. I'll grab it as soon
>   as I'm done with this.

50.

LEE puts the plate down. Then sits beside JESSIE.

> LEE
> Developing negs on the road.

> JESSIE
> Uh-huh. Got myself a pretty neat
> travel kit.

> LEE
> I'm impressed.

> JESSIE
> Want to know the secret of getting
> the developer just right?

JESSIE looks at LEE. Smiles.

Then unbuttons her shirt. And pulls out a white plastic
bottle of liquid that was pressed against her bare chest.

LEE sees a curve of breast.

> JESSIE (CONT'D)
> Body temperature.

JESSIE pulls her shirt closed.

> LEE
> ... Smart.

> JESSIE
> Thank you!

JESSIE uncaps the bottle, and starts pouring it carefully
into the tank.

> JESSIE (CONT'D)
> So - how about you tell me the
> story of how you became a
> photojournalist?

> LEE
> You don't know? I thought I was
> one of your heroes.

JESSIE laughs.

> JESSIE
> Yeah. I do. When you were at
> college, and took the
> motherfucking *legendary* photo of
> the ANTIFA massacre. Then became
> the youngest ever Magnum
> photographer.

51.

                    LEE
          I guess that would be my Wikipedia
          page.

                    JESSIE
          But what's it missing out?

                    LEE
          ... I don't know. A lot.

JESSIE sloshes the liquid around. Then puts the tank beside
her.

                    JESSIE
          Well, that's got to sit in there
          for ten minutes. So you may as
          well expand a little. What about
          your folks?

                    LEE
          Actually they're on a farm too.
          Except Colorado. Also pretending
          this isn't happening.

                    JESSIE
          No shit.

Beat.

JESSIE over looks at the roll of negs, hanging from the
handrail.

                    JESSIE (CONT'D)
          Hey. These are dry. Shall we
          check them out?

                    LEE
          Sure.

JESSIE pulls the strip down.

Then pulls a little lightbox from her pack, which has a clip
for her cellphone.

                    JESSIE
          Still need a phone, even though you
          can't get a signal.

JESSIE clips on her phone. Then hunches over, and starts
feeding the negs through the little lightbox. Using the
phone-camera to see the image.

                                                    52.

                    JESSIE (CONT'D)
          Oh my God. I don't want you to see
          these. They're all terrible.
          They're not even in focus...

                    LEE
          You were in combat.

                    JESSIE
          And the exposures are all wrong...

                    LEE
          Keep looking. I always figure the
          strike rate for keepers is about
          thirty-to-one.

JESSIE suddenly stops feeding the negs.

                    LEE (CONT'D)
          You found it, huh.

Silence.

Then JESSIE passes the lightbox to LEE.

LEE looks at the image on the phone screen.

It's a beautiful shot. Contrasty black and white, perfectly
framed, focused, and exposed - but horrific.

It's the CORPORAL attempting save SOLDIER MIKE. The fast
shutter speed freezes the blood jet from the neck. Black
suspended droplets hang in space like planets. The
CORPORAL'S face is desperate.

Around them, we can see the other SOLDIERS helplessly
watching.

A silent beat.

                    LEE (CONT'D)
          It's a great photo, Jessie.

LEE looks round at JESSIE.

JESSIE is staring straight ahead.

No longer proud or pleased with the photo. Lost in something
else. Overwhelmed. The shock of it. Sickened. Scared.

LEE hesitates.

Then puts a hand on JESSIE'S shoulder.

53.

                    LEE (CONT'D)
          I know.

Silence.

EXT. REFUGEE CAMP - NIGHT

Night, the REFUGEE CAMP.

Lights glowing in the tents. A few kids still playing in the
stands.

EXT. CAR - DAY

The SUV, driving through the landscape.

We are seeing more and more evidence of war.

Burned-out vehicles and buildings.

A family of refugees, pushing their worldly possessions in a
supermarket shopping cart.

Bodies, hung from overpass bridges.

Until -

EXT. TOWN/STREET - DAY

- SUDDENLY, and STRANGELY, the war-torn landscape gives way
to a total contrast.

The SUV is rolling down a street in a small town, which seems
to be completely untouched by any sign of conflict. As if it
is unaware of the war.

Nothing is blown up or burned out. No star-shaped shell
markings. No bullet holes.

A water sprinkler is running in a front garden.

A couple of young girls are walking with their mother.

A man is carrying bags of groceries.

INT. CAR - DAY

The journalists gaze out of the windows of the SUV.

                         JOEL
               ... Did we just drive through a
               time portal?

                         JESSIE
               It's the Twilight Zone.

EXT. TOWN/HIGH STREET - DAY

JOEL pulls up the car on the high street, outside a clothes
store.

The four journalists each get out of the SUV.

Look around.

An elderly woman walks past. Walking a small dog.

The dog yaps at JESSIE as it passes them.

INT. CLOTHES STORE - DAY

LEE, JESSIE and JOEL enter the clothes store.

A SHOP ASSISTANT is reading a book behind the counter.

                         SHOP ASSISTANT
               Hey there. Welcome. Feel free to
               look around.

                         LEE
               ... Appreciate it.

Beat.

                         JOEL
               Hey, out of interest, are you guys
               aware there's a... pretty huge
               civil war going on, across all
               America?

The SHOP ASSISTANT smiles.

                         SHOP ASSISTANT
               Oh sure. But we just try to stay
               out.

                         JOEL
               ... Stay out.

55.

                    SHOP ASSISTANT
          From what you see in the news,
          seems like it's for the best.

Beat.

                    SHOP ASSISTANT (CONT'D)
          Well, let me know if you want to
          try anything on. Men's on the
          left, women's on the right.

LEE clearly has zero intention of that.

But JESSIE does. She pulls out a summer dress from the rack.

She holds it up to herself, checking her reflection in the
mirror.

Then -

- turns to LEE.

                    JESSIE
          Lee. You got to put this on.

She holds it out to LEE.

LEE doesn't take it.

                    JESSIE (CONT'D)
          What - you're so war-torn you can't
          try on a dress?

CUT TO -

LEE standing in the summer dress.

Looking at herself in the mirror.

It's a strange transformation.

LEE is actually lost in it for a moment. It's like seeing
someone she used to know. Or hardly knew.

Then she notices JESSIE watching. Half smiling.

LEE laughs. A little embarrassed.

                    LEE
          Jesus. When you don't see yourself
          in a mirror for a few days.

                    JESSIE
          Oh my God. Shut the fuck up.

56.

JESSIE lifts her camera.

                    JESSIE (CONT'D)
          Turn around. I want to take your
          photo.

                    LEE
          No, come on.

                    JESSIE
          Yes!

A beat.

Then LEE turns.

Waits.

                    LEE
          ... Are you going to take the
          picture?

                    JESSIE
          You told me not to rush.

                    LEE
          Okay but there's a sweet spot. And
          you're missing it.

                    JESSIE
          I don't want to miss your sweet
          spot.

LEE is slightly taken aback. Was that an actual flirt?

At that moment - the snap of the shutter. JESSIE has taken
the photo.

                    LEE
          What? No - that was the wrong
          moment.

                    JESSIE
          Okay. One more.

JESSIE lifts the camera again.

                    JESSIE (CONT'D)
          Lee?

                    LEE
          Yes.

57.

> JESSIE
> You're pretty when you smile.

Involuntarily, LEE smiles.

Click.

> JESSIE (CONT'D)
> There ya go.

> JOEL
> Hey!

JESSIE and LEE look round.

JOEL'S found a hat. Has put it on. Rakish angle.

> JOEL (CONT'D)
> How about this?

JESSIE makes him wait a beat. Before teasing.

> JESSIE
> (flat)
> Yeah. Nice.

> JOEL
> ... You're not going to take a
> picture?

> JESSIE
> Right. You know what, though? I'm
> getting a little low on film.

LEE laughs.

> JOEL
> You're mean. I'm out.

He dumps the hat and exits.

JESSIE pulls out another dress.

> JESSIE
> Okay. I'm trying this one on.

EXT. TOWN/HIGH STREET - DAY

LEE exits the shop.

SAMMY is leaning against the SUV.

                    SAMMY
          You actually buy something?

                    LEE
          She did. Paying right now.

SAMMY smiles.

                    LEE (CONT'D)
          It's so weird. This place is like
          everything I'd forgotten.

                    SAMMY
          Funny. I was thinking it felt like
          everything I remembered.

SAMMY watches LEE.

                    SAMMY (CONT'D)
          Look at the tops of the buildings.
          Be subtle.

LEE turns. Looks up. As if checking the weather.

Sees - on the flat roofs of the high-street building -

- two men. Glimpses of their heads and shoulders. Black
sticks of rifle barrel.

Further down the high street, two more.

                    SAMMY (CONT'D)
          Wouldn't have suited us anyway,
          Lee. We'd have got bored.

INT. CAR - DAY

JOEL is driving.

SAMMY is in the front seat.

LEE is in the back with JESSIE.

LEE has her laptop open, balanced on her thighs, and is
editing photos.

On the radio, THE PRESIDENT is broadcasting.

                    THE PRESIDENT (O.S.)
          I remain ready to accept the full,
          immediate, and unconditional
          surrender of the Secessionist
          forces.
                    (MORE)

59.

>   THE PRESIDENT (O.S.) (CONT'D)
>   To liberate the people of the
>   subjugated states, and start
>   rebuilding our great nation: the
>   home of the free, and land of the -

SAMMY switches the radio off.

>   SAMMY
>   Enough of this shit. The words
>   might as well be random.

>   JOEL
>   What do you think he'll say if I do
>   get a mic in front of him?

SAMMY shrugs.

>   SAMMY
>   Not much. The ones that get taken -
>   Gaddafi, Mussolini, Ceauşesecu -
>   they're always lesser men than you
>   think.

SAMMY glances at JOEL.

>   SAMMY (CONT'D)
>   At the end, he'll let you down, Jo.

>   LEE
>   Just as long as he isn't dead
>   before I get there.

JOEL frowns.

>   JOEL
>   ... Hold up.

Then suddenly -

- he is braking. Slowing the vehicle fast.

The laptop nearly slides off LEE'S lap.

CUT TO -

EXT. COUNTRY ROAD - DAY

The flat landscape.

The one road.

The SUV is stopped on it.

60.

The fields either side.

In distance, on the far side of one of the fields, there is one building. A barn.

And a hundred yards ahead -

- something lying in the middle of the road.

LEE lifts her camera. Zoom lens fitted.

>   JOEL
>   ... Is it a body?

CUT TO -

- the view through LEE'S LENS.

It's definitely a body.

A dead soldier.

Flat on his back.

Head is blown to pieces.

Blood and brain are all over the road behind him.

CUT BACK TO -

- LEE.

Still looking through the lens.

>   LEE
>   Yeah.

>   JOEL
>   ... Shit.

JOEL switches the engine off.

They all listen.

Silence.

>   JOEL (CONT'D)
>   Can't hear anything.

Silence.

>   JOEL (CONT'D)
>   Can you see anything?

61.

LEE scans the landscape.

Aside from the distant barn, it's featureless.

> LEE
> Not aside from the body.

> SAMMY
> There was a turn-off three or four
> miles back. Maybe we should turn
> around. Find another route.

> JOEL
> You can't see *anything*? No
> movement at all? No shapes.

> LEE
> No.

Beat.

> JOEL
> Okay. I'm going to drive forward a
> little.

> LEE
> Slow.

> JOEL
> Yeah.

EXT. COUNTRY ROAD - DAY

Over the dead SOLDIER'S body -

- we watch the SUV crawl closer.

It gets within twenty feet.

Then stops again.

INT. CAR - DAY

JOEL looks at LEE.

> JOEL
> Shall we keep going -

> SPOTTER
> You don't want to be there.

A beat later -

62.

\- an impact noise.

The front windscreen is has been hit. And the pillar by JOEL'S window is impacted. A hole punched right through the metal.

A bullet has flown right past them.

A short, shocked beat. Then -

> JOEL
> *Fuck.*

\- JOEL floors the accelerator.

EXT. COUNTRY ROAD - DAY

The SUV jolts forwards -

\- bumps straight over the body of the dead SOLDIER -

\- and swerves towards the grass verge.

The only cover for two hundred yards in any direction.

Then it stops. Hard.

INT. CAR - DAY

JOEL and LEE exit the vehicle - fast.

JESSIE grabs her camera and pops her door.

> SAMMY
> Where you going?

> JESSIE
> ... With them.

> SAMMY
> Damn, girl. Don't be such a hotshot.

Beat.

> SAMMY (CONT'D)
> Just keep your head down.

> JESSIE
> No shit.

JESSIE slips out.

63.

And SAMMY lies himself flat on the seat.

EXT. COUNTRY ROAD/GRASS VERGE - DAY

JOEL edges along the side of the vehicle.

And sees -

- a few feet away from them, two soldiers, uniformed, lying prone. A SNIPER and a SPOTTER.

Their rifle is trained at a house, across the fields.

>   SPOTTER
>   Don't try driving on. This guy's a
>   good shot.

JOEL crawls up the verge towards the SNIPER and the SPOTTER.

JESSIE and LEE stay in the cover of the SUV.

The SPOTTER glances at them briefly.

Then goes back to his monocular.

>   JOEL
>   ... What's going on?

>   SPOTTER
>   Someone in that house. They're
>   stuck. We're stuck.

The man's voice is flat. Non-adrenalinised. Uninflected.

The SNIPER doesn't seem to be aware of their presence.

Purely concentrating on the view through his scope.

>   JOEL
>   ... Who do you think they are?

>   SPOTTER
>   No idea.

A sharp, snatched buzz sound.

Another round has flown by. Maybe a few feet away.

A beat later, a distant rifle shot.

The SNIPER flicks a bead of sweat off his head.

JOEL pulls out his press-pass necklace.

64.

                    JOEL
          ... We're press.

                    SPOTTER
          Cool. Now I understand why it's
          written on the side of your
          vehicle.

                    JOEL
          Are you WF? Who's giving you
          orders?

                    SPOTTER
          Nobody's giving us orders, man.
          Someone's trying to kill us. We're
          trying to kill them.

                    JOEL
          You don't know what side they're
          fighting for?

The SPOTTER keeps gazing through his monocular.

                    SPOTTER
          Oh, I get it. You're retarded.
          You don't understand a word I say.

He dips his monocular.

Turns to JESSIE.

                    SPOTTER (CONT'D)
          Yo. What's over there in that
          house?

                    JESSIE
          ... Someone shooting.

                    SPOTTER
              (to Joel)
          Complicated?

                    SNIPER
              (quiet, even)
          Yo. Guys. Shut the fuck up.

Everyone immediately falls quiet.

Silence.

Extends.

Wind noise.

65.

Grasses moving gently.

Breathing.

Where LEE lies, a beetle is climbing over a blade of grass. Right in front of her face.

She watches it. Gazes at the bright blue-green back.

Then suddenly -

- the SNIPER fires.

Everyone except the SNIPER and the SPOTTER flinch at the noise.

AT THIS MOMENT -

- JESSIE takes a photo.

Then the SNIPER relaxes his grip on his rifle.

>   SNIPER (CONT'D)
>   I got good news.

CUT TO -

EXT. SKY - DAY

- the SUN.

In a blue sky.

EXT. COUNTRY ROAD - DAY

The SUV drives down a road in open countryside.

Ahead is forest.

INT. CAR - DAY

Inside the car, positions have switched.

JOEL is in the front passenger seat, asleep.

LEE is driving.

JESSIE is half dozing. Her head keeps dropping.

SAMMY nudges her.

66.

                    JOEL
          Hey. Why don't you put your head
          down there. Take it from an old
          hand - you never know what's coming
          around the next corner.

                    JESSIE
          All right.

JESSIE curls up on the back seat.

Closes her eyes.

EXT. COUNTRY ROAD - DAY

The car enters forest.

REVEAL -

- some distance back from the SUV, there is one other
vehicle.

Travelling in the same direction.

INT. CAR - DAY

JESSIE is asleep.

JOEL is asleep.

LEE keeps checking her rear-view mirror.

                    LEE
          Sammy.

SAMMY immediately catches LEE'S tone.

                    SAMMY
          What?

                    LEE
          We've got a car coming up on us
          pretty fast.

SAMMY checks through the rear window.

Sees the vehicle through the rear window.

The road through the forest is snaking -

- but as the road straightens, we see the following white car
rounding the corner behind.

67.

It's halved the distance since we first saw it, and is
closing quickly.

                    SAMMY
          ... What do you think?

                    LEE
          I don't know.

                    SAMMY
          Maybe they're just in a hurry.

                    LEE
          Oh, they're in a hurry. He smoked
          his tyres on the last corner.

EXT. COUNTRY ROAD - DAY

The vehicle keeps closing on the SUV.

INT. CAR - DAY

                    SAMMY
          Okay. Well, we're not outrunning
          anyone in this thing. So slow down
          a little, Lee. Let them pass.

                    LEE
          Roger that.

                    SAMMY
          Don't look out at them. We just
          let them roll by.

EXT. FOREST ROAD - DAY

The vehicle is now almost on their bumper.

Then it pulls out. Starts to overtake.

But as it draws alongside, it holds speed.

With them.

Then starts honking its horn.

INT. CAR - DAY

The noise wakes JOEL and JESSIE.

68.

> SAMMY
>
> Oh fuck. Here we go.

But LEE - who *has* looked out at them - suddenly bursts out laughing.

Reveal -

- in the car alongside is TONY - the Chinese journalist from New York.

He's in the passenger seat, with the window down. Waving and grinning.

The driver is BOHAI.

EXT. CARS/SIDE BY SIDE - DAY

JOEL winds down his window. TONY and JOEL shout at each other over the wind noise.

> JOEL
>
> Holy shit, Tony! What the fuck?

> TONY
>
> How you doing, guys?

> JOEL
>
> You just scared the shit out of us!
> Coming up like that!

> TONY
>
> Good! That was the idea!

> JOEL
>
> What are you doing here?

> TONY
>
> I don't know, Jo! What are you
> doing here?

JOEL laughs.

> JOEL
>
> Fuck you!

INT. CAR - DAY

JOEL turns to SAMMY.

> JOEL
>
> Can you believe these guys?

                    SAMMY
          Yeah, I can.

                    JOEL
          Small world.

                    SAMMY
          Small world my ass. They were
          following us. Did you tell them
          where you were heading, back in New
          York?

                    JOEL
          Fuck no!

LEE looks of her window -

EXT. CARS/SIDE BY SIDE - DAY

- and shouts to TONY.

                    LEE
          Tony! Did Jo tell you where we
          were going, back in New York?

                    TONY
          He was pretty drunk, Lee. When he
          was hitting on that girl you got in
          the back seat.

INT. CAR - DAY

SAMMY shakes his head.

                    LEE
          You're a dick.

                    JOEL
          Oh man. I must have been so
          wasted.

TONY shouts over to them.

                    TONY
          Hey!

                    LEE
               (shouts back)
          What?

70.

EXT. CARS/SIDE BY SIDE - DAY

TONY shouts.

> TONY
> I'm done with Bohai! He's lousy
> company, and he drives like a
> maniac!

> BOHAI
> (in Mandarin)
> *What did you just say?*

> TONY
> (in Mandarin)
> *You drive like a grandmother.*

TONY starts climbing out of the passenger window.

> TONY (CONT'D)
> I'm coming over to your car.

INT. CAR - DAY

JOEL looks over. Sees TONY half out of his window.

> JESSIE
> What the *fuck*?

> TONY
> *Keep the car steady!*

> LEE
> Are you crazy, Tony!

> TONY
> *Just keep the car steady, Lee!*

TONY'S hand reaches out to grab the window frame of the back
seat.

EXT. CARS/SIDE BY SIDE - DAY

TONY shouts to BOHAI.

> TONY
> (in Mandarin)
> *Closer!*

BOHAI steers, closing the gap.

TONY lunges forwards through the open window.

INT. CAR - DAY

JESSIE tries to make herself small, as TONY clambers over her, laughing hysterically.

>   JESSIE
>   (laughing)
>   That's sick! That's so sick!

>   JOEL
>   You crazy bastard, Tony!

TONY half falls into the footwell.

>   JESSIE
>   I'm doing it!

>   LEE
>   What?

>   JESSIE
>   I gotta do it.

The next moment, JESSIE is climbing out of the rear passenger window.

>   JOEL
>   Jesus! *Lee* -

>   LEE
>   Yeah - I see!

>   JOEL
>   Don't fucking turn the wheel!

>   LEE
>   There's a *corner* coming up!

But the next moment, JESSIE has pulled herself through.

Her feet slip out the window, and she's gone.

EXT. CARS/SIDE BY SIDE - DAY

JESSIE pops up in the back of BOHAI'S car, grinning and laughing.

BOHAI shouts across.

>   BOHAI
>   My new passenger - much better!
>   Much better!

                         TONY
              Fuck you!

                         BOHAI
              Bye-bye, Tony! Bye-bye! See you
              in Washington!

Then BOHAI floors it.

INT. CAR - DAY

BOHAI'S car accelerates fast away from the SUV.

Disappearing almost immediately around the next corner.

TONY has sat himself up in the back seat.

                         TONY
              Told you he drives like a maniac.

LEE accelerates -

- but the SUV won't take it.

It's not just slower than the other - it's heavier. On the
next corner, it understeers, pulling out to the outside.

                         SAMMY
              What the fuck! Slow down!

LEE eases up.

And when they come out of the corner -

- BOHAI'S car is nowhere to be seen.

TONY is still laughing.

But LEE is not.

All the humour is draining out of her.

EXT. FOREST ROAD - DAY

The SUV turns another corner.

The road ahead is still empty.

INT. CAR - DAY

JOEL frowns.

                    JOEL
          Where did they go?

                    SAMMY
               (to Lee)
          This feel funny?

                    LEE
          Like what kind?

                    SAMMY
          I don't know. Not right.

                    LEE
          I agree. I don't like this at all.
               (to Tony)
          Where'd your guy go, Tony?

                    TONY
          He's just fucking around, that's
          all.

                    LEE
          I don't want him fucking around.
          I want Jessie back in this car.

                    TONY
          Relax, Lee. He's just showing how
          fast he can drive. The girl is
          fine.

                    LEE
               (suddenly snaps)
          How the fuck do you know if she's
          fine? Can you see her?

TONY is shocked.

                    TONY
          Hey - cool it! I'm just saying.
          She's - fine.

At that moment -

- the thick trees of the forest break.

The car is cresting the top of a hill, from which the road
winds down.

And as it crests -

- it reveals BOHAI'S CAR, a little distance ahead.

It's pulled up on the side of the road, on the lawn in front of a farmhouse.

Beyond the farmhouse is a BARN.

LEE brakes.

The car stops.

They stare at the sight of the abandoned car for a beat.

> SAMMY
> ... Shit.

EXT. BARN - DAY

LEE, JOEL, TONY and SAMMY have moved up to the side of the BARN.

Around the back of the BARN, two hundred metres away, there is a construction site, of sorts.

CUT TO -

- LEE. Mounting a 24-240mm zoom onto her camera.

CUT TO -

EXT. MASS GRAVE - DAY

- THE VIEW THROUGH THE ZOOM LENS.

Off the road, a digger has excavated a large trench in the earth.

The digger is being operated by a SOLDIER.

Inside the trench, there are stacked bodies. Could be fifty. Could be more.

A dump truck is backed up to the trench - and the back is lifting.

Bodies are sliding into the pit.

The lens REFRAMES -

- and finds two more SOLDIERS, standing by the side of the trench.

BOHAI and JESSIE are standing in front of them, arms raised.

75.

EXT. BARN - DAY

LEE lowers the lens.

She looks ashen.

Beat.

>   LEE
>   We need to go down there. Now.

>   SAMMY
>   (flat)
>   Lee. If we go down there, they're
>   going to kill us.

>   JOEL
>   What? Sammy, no. Those aren't
>   government forces. Not out here.
>   We're cool. We got our press
>   passes.

>   LEE
>   Jessie doesn't.

>   JOEL
>   But we do. We're fine. Let's go.

JOEL starts to rise.

But SAMMY catches his arm.

>   SAMMY
>   You're not listening to me. Those
>   people do not want to have been
>   seen doing what they're doing.

LEE lifts her camera again.

THROUGH THE ZOOM LENS -

- she can see that JESSIE and BOHAI have been put into a
kneeling position, with their hands on their heads.

The two SOLDIERS are apparently in discussion.

>   JOEL
>   Tell us, Lee.

>   LEE
>   They've got them both kneeling.
>   They're talking.

                                                    76.

                    JOEL
          Kneeling is not good.

                    TONY
          They're probably just giving them a
          scare. They're not going to shoot
          anyone.

                    SAMMY
          They killed all the people in that
          fucking ditch. That could be a
          whole town. But they'll stop now?

                    TONY
          Who knows where those bodies are
          from?

                    SAMMY
          Are the bodies in uniform?

                    LEE
          No. They aren't.

LEE lowers the camera again.

Rises.

                    LEE (CONT'D)
          I've got to go.

                    JOEL
          I'm coming with you.

                    TONY
          Me too.

                    SAMMY
          Jesus. I'm telling you, *every*
          instinct in me says - this is
          death. Okay? Death.

LEE turns to SAMMY.

                    LEE
          You stay. You *stay*. Because
          you're too old. And you can't run.

She's not being cruel. She's being hard.

A beat between SAMMY and LEE.

                    SAMMY
          Oh fuck. Fuck this.

77.

LEE starts walking.

EXT. MASS GRAVE - DAY

LEE, JOEL, and TONY walk in a line, side by side, down
towards the mass grave.

As they walk, they are spotted by the two SOLDIERS. Who turn
to watch them approach.

>   LEE
>   (quiet)
>   Who's doing the talking?

>   JOEL
>   (quiet)
>   Me.

>   LEE
>   (quiet)
>   Okay.

As they near the SOLDIERS, JOEL lifts his hand.

Puts a big smile on his face.

>   JOEL
>   Hey guys. What's happening?

JESSIE and BOHAI turn their heads.

JESSIE looks at straight at LEE. She looks terrified.

Neither of the SOLDIERS reply to JOEL'S question.

Just silently watch the group of journalists complete the
remainder of the distance.

Once the journalists reach the SOLDIERS, JOEL tries again.

>   JOEL (CONT'D)
>   So. Looks like we've got some kind
>   of misunderstanding here.

One of the SOLDIERS steps forwards.

>   SOLDIER
>   Yeah?

>   JOEL
>   Yes, sir. Those two guys there,
>   they're my colleagues.

                              SOLDIER
                    What kind of colleagues.

                                JOEL
                    Journalists, sir.

JOEL reaches into his shirt. Pulls out his PRESS ID
necklace.

                           JOEL (CONT'D)
                    We're actually just passing
                    through.

The SOLDIER just stares at JOEL.

His face is dead. Not angry. Not wired.

But it's the deadness that makes him feel so dangerous.

                              SOLDIER
                    Passing through to where?

                                JOEL
                    Charlottesville.

                              SOLDIER
                    What's in Charlottesville?

JOEL smiles again.

                                JOEL
                    Good hiking, I hear.

Silence.

JOEL'S smile drops. He keeps trying to force the
casualness. The no need for concern.

But he can feel it failing as he speaks. They all can.

                           JOEL (CONT'D)
                    We're actually covering the ah -
                    the university campus there? Which
                    has apparently started a programme
                    toreopen the school. It's a real
                    feel-good story. And, ah - we all
                    need that, right?

Silence.

Then the SOLDIER brings his gun round to point at BOHAI.

                              SOLDIER
                    This guy here is your colleague.

                    JOEL
          Yes, sir. He is.

                    SOLDIER
          This guy.

                    JOEL
          Yes, sir.

Almost instantly, the SOLDIER pulls the trigger.

Shoots BOHAI in the head.

He flops down.

JESSIE involuntarily screams.

                    SOLDIER
          That guy.

A beat of pure shock.

The strange acceleration of a moment in time, from one space,
to a completely different space.

JOEL starts to speak again.

His instinct is still to try to sound somehow reasonable.
Calm. But he's not able to make a sentence.

                    JOEL
          Okay. So. Okay - please. Just -
          please -

                    SOLDIER
          'Just please.' Just what.

                    JOEL
          Sir, we're -

                    SOLDIER
          - Sir, yes?

                    JOEL
          - American journalists.

                    SOLDIER
          You said that already.

                    JOEL
          We work for Reuters.

                    SOLDIER
          Reuters doesn't sound American.

80.

                    JOEL
          It's -

JOEL doesn't know what to say.

He glances down. Sees a huge pool of blood spreading from
BOHAI'S head. Pushing into the dust.

                    JOEL (CONT'D)
          - It's a news agency.

                    SOLDIER
          I know what Reuters is.

                    JOEL
          Sir - I'm just saying we're
          American.

                    SOLDIER
          Okay. And which bit of American
          are you? Central American? South
          American?

Beat.

                    JOEL
          ... Florida.

                    SOLDIER
          Florida. Central.

JESSIE is hyperventilating.

The SOLDIER turns his attention to her.

                    SOLDIER (CONT'D)
          And where are you from?

JESSIE can hardly speak, she's so scared.

                    LEE
               (quiet, firm)
          Answer him, Jessie.

                    JESSIE
          Missouri.

The SOLDIER nods.

                    SOLDIER
          Missouri. Okay. Now that is
          American. Hundred per cent.

He turns to LEE.

SOLDIER (CONT'D)
You?

Beat.

LEE
Colorado.

SOLDIER
Missouri and Colorado. Now we're
talking.

He turns to TONY.

SOLDIER (CONT'D)
You?

TONY swallows.

Says nothing.

SOLDIER (CONT'D)
What? You don't speak? Are you
mute?

Silence.

SOLDIER (CONT'D)
Can't speak English?

Silence.

The SOLDIER lifts his gun.

Points it at TONY'S chest.

SOLDIER (CONT'D)
You'd better speak English.

TONY catches his breath. Swallows again.

Then speaks. Shaking.

TONY
I'm from Hong Kong.

SOLDIER
Oh. China.

Beat.

Then the SOLDIER repeats the word.

Kind of spits it out.

SOLDIER (CONT'D)
China.

Then without a further hesitation, shoots into TONY'S chest.

JESSIE screams again.

TONY falls back. Gurgles. Mouth filling with blood. His arms flap.

LEE
FUCK -

JOEL
(shouts)
SIR - NO! PLEASE! NO! DO NOT!

SOLDIER
(shouts back)
DO NOT? DO NOT? IS THAT A FUCKING ORDER?

He lifts his gun and points it at JOEL.

JESSIE keeps screaming.

Loud. Helpless. Uncontrolled.

JOEL
PLEASE DON'T -

The combined noise is so loud -

- that no one hears the noise of a car engine.

Until it's too nearly on them.

And at that moment, everyone turns -

- to see SAMMY driving the SUV. Fast. From the side. Right at them.

SOLDIER
What the fuck -

Too late.

The SUV ploughs straight into the SOLDIER. And the other, beside him.

It misses JESSIE, LEE and JOEL by a couple of feet.

The two SOLDIERS are knocked sideways.

One of them impacts JESSIE –

– and knocks her sideways INTO the MASS GRAVE.

The SUV slams on the brakes.

Skids to halt.

LEE turns to look for JESSIE –

– and she is gone.

The space where she knelt is empty.

CUT TO –

– JESSIE.

In bodies of the MASS GRAVE.

Stunned.

Then –

– crawling over the bodies, to the edge of the pit.

CUT TO –

– JESSIE appearing over the lip. Trying to pull herself up.

Then –

– being DRAGGED UPWARDS by JOEL.

>   SAMMY
>   (screams)
>   *GET IN – GET IN!*

LEE, JESSIE, and JOEL scramble for the SUV.

As they get through the doors –

– the SOLDIER in the digger is jumping out of the cabin.

As the SUV accelerates away, skidding onto the road –

– the SOLDIER lifts his rifle.

Aims at the departing vehicle, as it passes almost parallel
to him.

Fifty metres distant.

The SOLDIER fires.

84.

The SUV doesn't stop. Vanishes into the treeline.

INT. CAR - NIGHT

The car drives fast through forest.

JESSIE is throwing up in the back seat.

LEE is beside JESSIE, clutching the seat in front. As if trying to anchor herself.

JOEL is hyperventilating.

And SAMMY is looking dazed.

No one says anything.

The only noise is the sound of the car engine, and JESSIE retching.

Then -

SAMMY speaks.

>   SAMMY
>   We've got to stop.

>   JOEL
>   ... What are you talking about?

>   SAMMY
>   I can't drive.

LEE is staring across at SAMMY.

>   LEE
>   Jo -

>   JOEL
>   We *can't* stop. You've *got* to
>   fucking drive.

>   SAMMY
>   I can't.

>   LEE
>   *JO!* He's been *hit*! He's bleeding!

JOEL looks down. Sees SAMMY'S waist is completely soaked with blood.

>   JOEL
>   Oh *fuck*.

85.

SAMMY'S expression - he's getting woozy. Fast.

>   JOEL (CONT'D)
> No, no, *no* -

>   SAMMY
>   (slurs)
> Got to stop -

SAMMY puts the brakes on.

Stops the car.

Opens the door.

Tries to get out.

Almost immediately collapses.

LEE gets out to help him -

- as JOEL clambers into the driver seat.

LEE helps the bigger, heavier, older man into the back seat.

SAMMY collapses sideways as he sits.

Lee gets into the front seat.

>   LEE
> Go!

JOEL accelerates.

CUT TO -

- JESSIE.

Wide-eyed. Lost in shock and madness of it all.

EXT. FOREST ROAD - NIGHT

The car drives.

Winds along the twisting road.

Gradually, as it drives -

- something starts to be seen through the forest trees.

An orange glow.

INT. CAR - NIGHT

SAMMY - drifting close to the edge of consciousness - lifts his eyes.

To look out the window.

Sees the orange glow.

> SAMMY
> (quiet)
> ... A forest fire.

Beat.

> SAMMY (CONT'D)
> (quiet)
> How fucking strange...

No one seems to hear.

JOEL just keeps driving.

Gaze fixed on the road ahead.

EXT. FOREST ROAD - NIGHT

The car drives fast.

Burning trees either side of the road.

Behind the vehicle, sparks are in the slipstream. They whirl into patterns.

We let the car pull away.

And we stay on the empty road, as the fire builds.

EXT. RIVANNA RIVER - SUNRISE

Aerial shot.

Near Charlottesville, 120 miles from Washington DC.

The RIVANNA River.

EXT. RIVANNA RIVER/WESTERN FORCES MILITARY BASE - SUNRISE

By the river, a military base.

Tents. Tanks. Trucks. SAMs. APCs. Jeeps.

87.

Overhead, Chinooks and Apaches.

EXT. WESTERN FORCES MILITARY BASE/MEDICAL TENTS - SUNRISE

The SUV is parked by a medical tent.

SILENCE THROUGH LEE'S LENS

SAMMY leans against the car window.

His eyes are open.

Sightless.

JESSIE is standing outside the car.

Dazed. Staring at him.

EXT. WESTERN FORCES MILITARY BASE/VEHICLES - DAY

A helicopter passes overhead.

LEE has found a place to sit alone.

She's looking through photos on the back of her camera.

She hovers over the photo of Sammy, dead.

She stares at it.

Her eyes fill.

But she doesn't weep.

She wipes the tears away.

Then brings up the delete option on the photo.

Presses delete.

Is offered the option - yes or no.

Pauses.

Beat.

Then chooses no.

EXT. WESTERN FORCES MILITARY BASE/TENTS - DAY

LEE walks through the camp.

Alone.

Until she sees what she's half looking for.

JOEL.

He's leaning against a jeep. His vodka bottle is mostly empty. He's smoking weed.

With him are DAVE, the TV journalist from New York, and his TV REPORTER, ANYA.

They're both in military uniform - but wear blue Kevlar over the khaki, with PRESS written in large letters on the front and back.

They look round as LEE reaches them.

>   ANYA
> God. We just heard about Sammy.

>   DAVE
> And the other two guys.

>   JOEL
> Tony. Bohai. Their names.

>   ANYA
> Yeah. Christ. Lee - I'm really
> sorry. I know what he was to you.

>   DAVE
> It's so fucked up.

>   JOEL
> Oh, it's *so* fucked up.
>   (to Lee)
> Wait until you hear what these two
> embedded motherfuckers have to say.

Beat.

>   JOEL (CONT'D)
> What? Tell her.

>   ANYA
> You know what, Jo? I'm trying to
> talk to Lee about Sammy.

>   JOEL
> I heard - your condolences. Means
> a lot. Now tell her.

ANYA pointedly ignores JOEL.

                    ANYA
               (to Lee)
          We loved Sammy too. Everyone did.

                    LEE
          Thanks, Anya.

                    JOEL
               (cuts in)
          For fuck's sake. The Western
          Forces are moving in to DC tonight.
          Earlier today, the government
          military basically surrendered.

LEE looks at ANYA.

                    ANYA
          ... Yeah. It's true.

                    DAVE
          DC's only protection now is a few
          do-or-die soldiers and a handful of
          Secret Service. The WF will roll
          right in.

                    JOEL
               (to Lee)
          So you and me are too late. We
          missed the story. And Sammy didn't
          even die for anything good.

Silence.

                    ANYA
          ... I think we'll give you guys
          some space.

They turn to go.

DAVE taps LEE'S arm as he goes.

                    DAVE
          Truly sorry.

LEE and JOEL are left alone.

Silence.

EXT. RIVANNA RIVER/BANKS - DAY

LEE walks long the riverbank, looking for JESSIE.

A little way down, she finds her.

90.

Sitting on the banks. FE2s by her side.

EXT. RIVANNA RIVER/BANKS - DAY

JESSIE looks round as LEE sits beside her.

They sit in silence for a beat.

> JESSIE
> Where's Jo.

> LEE
> Processing.

> JESSIE
> Me too.

Beat.

> JESSIE (CONT'D)
> I hardly knew Sammy, compared to
> you, but -

> LEE
> - No, you knew him. The guy you
> saw. That's who he was.

LEE hesitates.

> LEE (CONT'D)
> There's so many ways it could have
> ended for him. A lot of them were
> worse.

Beat.

> LEE (CONT'D)
> He didn't want to quit.

Silence.

> JESSIE
> You know, when we were by the
> helicopter, I didn't really
> understand what you were saying.
> But -
>   (beat)
> These last few days, I've never
> been scared like that before. And
> I've never felt more alive.

LEE looks at JESSIE.

91.

And understands.

JESSIE'S not going to quit either.

EXT. WESTERN FORCES MILITARY BASE - DAY

A deafening noise.

A Chinook flying directly overhead.

Beneath it, JOEL is startled awake, from where he'd been out cold on the ground beside the SUV.

He sits up.

The sky is full of helicopters.

A line of infantry trucks driving right past.

One passes. Two. Three.

And in the third, he sees DAVE and ANYA sat in the back.

ANYA sees JOEL.

JOEL holds up a hand.

ANYA does the same.

Then they are gone.

EXT. WESTERN FORCES MILITARY BASE - DAY

Dejected, beaten, JOEL walks across to the SUV.

JESSIE is by the back of the SUV, loading film.

Another deafening helicopter flies directly overhead.

JOEL walks around to the side of the SUV.

And finds -

- LEE is using a bucket and cloth to wipe SAMMY'S blood off the back seats.

He immediately understands.

They're going to DC.

LEE looks up.

92.

Sees him.

As their eyes lock –

CUT TO –

EXT. WASHINGTON – NIGHT

– HELICOPTER GUNSHIPS flying over DC.

In places, the city is burning.

Tracer-fire sine-waves curve into the sky.

We fly over the PENTAGON, towards the Potomac and the LINCOLN MEMORIAL.

CUT TO –

EXT. LINCOLN MEMORIAL – NIGHT

– LEE.

She's clutching her camera.

But not taking photos.

She's frozen.

REVEAL –

– SOLDIERS, crouched behind armoured vehicles, positioned at the base of the LINCOLN MEMORIAL.

The air is crackling with rifle and machine-gun fire.

JESSIE is photographing.

A ROCKET is fired from the LINCOLN MEMORIAL –

It flies past the vehicles and EXPLODES a KIOSK in the park behind them.

The DETONATION rips through the trees.

In reply –

– a SOLDIER with a JAVELIN moves around the side of the vehicle.

Brings the weapon up.

93.

Then fires.

Around him, dust from the road jumps into air, shrouding him.

CUT TO -

EXT. LINCOLN MEMORIAL - NIGHT

- the rocket flying between two pillars on the left side of the LINCOLN MEMORIAL.

The explosion shakes the structure.

Smoke and fire balloon out around the pillars either side.

CUT TO -

- JESSIE taking the shot.

Winding the film.

Eyes bright. Wide.

Knowing the shot she just took was iconic.

Knowing she got it right.

CUT TO -

EXT. WASHINGTON/17TH STREET - NIGHT

- the JOURNALISTS moving north up 17th Street -

- following a squad of SOLDIERS.

On the FAR SIDE of the road, another squad is also moving north.

Ahead, blocking the road, is a makeshift barricade of parked cars.

As the FAR-SIDE SQUAD reach the barricade, and start to edge past it -

- a hidden IED explodes.

MOMENTS LATER -

- WASHINGTON DEFENDERS open fire from two positions in the buildings ahead. A crossfire.

94.

The JOURNALISTS and the NEAR-SIDE SQUAD run for cover - tothe PILLARS of an office building ahead.

Surviving soldiers from the FAR-SIDE SQUAD take cover behindcar barricade.

For several beats -

- sustained gunfire, hitting glass, metal, and concrete.

JESSIE and JOEL catch each other's gaze.

The gaze locks.

Just recognising. Where they are, what is happening.

CUT TO -

- LEE.

In the opposite space.

She's shut down. Staring.

Overwhelmed by horror.

Overwhelmed by the deafening, jarring noise of battle, echoing around the canyon of buildings.

THROUGH THE NOISE -

- the sound of a HELICOPTER.

Engine blast.

FLYING IN from the SOUTH.

FIRING ROCKETS at the WASHINGTON DEFENDER POSITIONS.

The HELICOPTER flares.

Hovers.

Directly ABOVE the barricade.

Rotor wash blasts through the pillars where the JOURNALISTS hide.

BENEATH the HELICOPTER -

- the FAR-SIDE SQUAD scatter -

- as a TANK and HUMVEES approach.

And SMASH THROUGH the barricade.

The NEAR-SIDE SQUAD move out.

CUT TO -

JESSIE.

Moving. Shooting. Winding.

CUT TO -

LEE.

Falling further into herself.

LEE is breaking.

It is as if the more JESSIE ascends, the more LEE descends.

EXT. ROOFTOPS - NIGHT

ON ROOFTOPS -

- WESTERN FORCES SNIPER and MORTAR TEAMS take positions.

As a MORTAR TEAM FIRES, **CUT TO -**

EXT. WASHINGTON/BARRICADE - NIGHT

- the sound of MORTAR SHELLS landing around the WHITE HOUSE.

- which is on the far side of a high and gated CONCRETE
BARRICADE, blocking Pennsylvania Avenue.

LEE, JESSIE and JOEL huddle up by the corner of a building.

JOEL looks around the corner, and SEES -

- the BARRICADE.

- a SQUAD of WF SOLDIERS in a firefight with DEFENDER
SOLDIERS, who are positioned by the RECESSED GATE, behind
HESCO BARRIERS and inside a CONCRETE TOWER.

JOEL pulls back.

> JESSIE
> Can you see it?

> JOEL
> Take a look.

96.

They swap.

JESSIE glimpses.

> JESSIE
> ... Oh my God - we're so fucking
> close.

Two HUMVEES roll past them.

Tucked behind the nearest HUMVEE are a SQUAD of WF SOLDIERS, led by SERGEANT JO.

LEE stares blankly at the same sight.

JOEL grabs her.

> JOEL
> Come on, Lee - we're nearly there -
> *move*.

ACTION SEQUENCE:

UNDER CONSTANT FIRE, and SOUND OF MORTARS, and HELICOPTERS, and SURROUNDING FIREFIGHTS -

- the JOURNALISTS fall inside behind SERGEANT JO SQUAD and HUMVEE 1, as -

- HUMVEE 2 ACCELERATES to protect the WF SQUAD, caught in the firefight.

- HUMVEE 1 and HUMVEE 2 open fire on GATE DEFENDERS.

- HUMVEE 2 is blown up by a rocket, fired from the TOWER.

- HUMVEE 1 reverses, leaving SERGEANT JO SQUAD and the JOURNALISTS exposed.

- Two TANKS are rolling in.

- TANK 1 blows up the TOWER.

- TANK 2 fires at the GATE.

- SERGEANT JO SQUAD kill remaining GATE DEFENDERS.

- TANK 2 moves forwards.

- SERGEANT JO SQUAD fall in behind TANK 2.

- JOURNALISTS fall in behind TANK 2.

- JOURNALISTS take position behind HESCO BARRIER.

97.

\- TANK 2 smashes through the GATE.

REVEALING -

\- the WHITE HOUSE.

CUT TO -

\- JESSIE, moving up from cover at the HESCO BARRIER, lifting her camera.

PHOTOGRAPHING TANK 2.

Around TANK 2, we can see the DAMAGE to the area surrounding the WHITE HOUSE.

MORTAR IMPACTS, broken fence, craters, abandoned vehicles.

JESSIE sees as JOEL drags LEE to cover.

LEE seems now fully broken.

JESSIE stares at LEE - in disbelief.

Almost with contempt.

LEE and JESSIE have now almost fully traded places.

JUST AHEAD OF THEM -

\- SOLDIERS have moved to the smashed gate.

Now only a couple of hundred yards from the WHITE HOUSE entrance.

>   SOLDIER
>   The Beast. Two Suburbans. Right
>   outside.

CUT TO -

\- ANYA, in full flak and defensive gear, but oddly glamorous -

\- facing us, talking into camera.

>   ANYA
>   Western Forces have now surrounded
>   the White House, where the
>   President is still believed to be.
>   We are approaching from
>   Pennsylvania Avenue, where -

ANYA is interrupted by RAPID SEQUENCE of MORTAR SHELL EXPLOSIONS, and a ROAR of HELICPTER NOISE.

                              98.

                    ANYA (CONT'D)
                 (over the noise)
            Shit - we need to go again.

REVEAL -

- this is a PIECE TO CAMERA.

ANYA and DAVE have moved up, and are close to LEE, JOEL, and
JESSIE. Just the other side of the RECESSED GATE.

                         JOEL
                    (seeing them)
                 - Motherfuckers.

DAVE dips his CAMERA.

Calls across to LEE and JOEL.

He's as wired as they are. But weirdly conversational.

                         DAVE
            Lee, Lee, knows where to be. You
            getting good shit?

LEE doesn't seem to hear him.

JOEL covers for her.

                         JOEL
            Lincoln Memorial. You?

                         DAVE
            WF rappelling off a chopper to the
            Pentagon roof.

DAVE takes the glimpse around the corner to the WHITE HOUSE.

He pulls back.

                    DAVE (CONT'D)
            But there's only one shot. Right,
            Lee?

                         JOEL
            You really think he's in there?

                         DAVE
            WF have intel from the generals
            that surrendered yesterday. He's
            right in that fucking building.

JESSIE looks towards the WHITE HOUSE.

99.

              JESSIE
   Fuck.

              JOEL
   What do you hear they're going to
   do with him?

              DAVE
   Kill. No capture. It's whoever
   gets a gun to his head first. Hey,
   Lee - don't beat me to the money
   shot, okay?

ANYA taps DAVE.

              ANYA
   Dave - going again.

As DAVE RESHOULDERS HIS CAMERA -

- JOEL sees something.

By the WHITE HOUSE, SECRET SERVICE suddenly POURING out of
the WHITE HOUSE entrance - surrounding and propelling SOMEONE
into the BEAST.

              JOEL
   ... Jesus. It's happening.

             SOLDIER
   He's busting out!

ACTION SEQUENCE:

- the BEAST and TWO SUBURBANS, accelerating towards the
BARRICADE.

- GUNFIRE erupting.

- WF HELICOPTER above, moving in, firing.

- the BEAST and SUBURBANS swerving either side of TANK 2.

- accelerating towards the BROKEN GATE.

- LEAD SUBURBAN, in a hail of bullets, smashes into HUMVEE 2.

- BEAST flashes BETWEEN LEE, JOEL, JESSIE, and ANYA and DAVE.

- REAR SUBURBAN smashes into the TOWER.

- SECRET SERVICE exit HUMVEE 2 and are immediately shot by
SERGEANT JO SQUAD.

100.

- REVEAL HUMVEE 3, moving fast.

- HUMVEE 3 makes hard side impact into the BEAST, just as it is about to swerve TANK 1.

- BEAST is pinned.

- HUMVEE 1 moves forwards, firing into the side of the BEAST.

- WF SOLDIERS emerge from everywhere, converging on the BEAST.

- SERGEANT JO SQUAD move in.

- DAVE and ANYA move in, DAVE filming ANYA.

>   ANYA
>   (to camera)
>   The President's vehicle has been
>   stopped by Western Forces as it
>   attempted to escape -

CUT TO -

JESSIE. Stunned.

>   JESSIE
>   ... Whoa.

CUT TO -

- LEE.

As if the BEAST screaming past them has jolted.

She stands.

Staring at the WHITE HOUSE.

Coming back to life.

Like a prizefighter. Knocked out. Picking themselves up off the canvas, only out of the fighter's instinct, for one last round.

CUT TO -

JOEL.

He starts to move towards the BEAST -

- then is stopped.

LEE has caught his arm.

                    LEE
          He's not there.

                    JOEL
          ... What?

                    LEE
          He's not there, Jo.

JOEL stares at her.

Knows that *she* knows.

LEE starts walking.

Then running.

But not towards the BEAST.

Towards the WHITE HOUSE.

A beat.

JOEL looks back towards the BEAST.

Sees DAVE and ANYA - closing in on the BEAST, as it is
relentlessly shot by HUMVEE 1 and the approaching WF FORCES.

                    JOEL
          Fuck.

Beat.

                    JOEL (CONT'D)
               (to Jessie)
          Come on.

Then he starts after LEE, and JESSIE follows.

CUT TO -

EXT. WHITE HOUSE - NIGHT

- the three journalists, running to the WHITE HOUSE.

INT. THE WHITE HOUSE/ENTRANCE HALL - NIGHT

LEE, JOEL, and JESSIE walk into the entrance hall.

In the distance, the sounds of sustained gunfire and
HELICOPTERS continue.

102.

Ahead of them are open doors, with a window to the South
Lawn.

A beat, as they all gaze around.

After the chaos of outside, the stillness and the grandeur
are surreal.

Their footsteps on the marble floor.

The slight echo to their voices.

JESSIE walks up to the open doors of the room ahead.

Inside, lying on a Persian rug, there are two bodies.

A MAN and a WOMAN.

The WOMAN is face-down. The MAN is face-up. Both are shot
in the head.

Their pools of blood connect.

A hand gun is on the floor.

JESSIE takes a picture.

INT. THE WHITE HOUSE/PIANO ROOM - NIGHT

LEE, JOEL and JESSIE enter a large room with a GRAND PIANO.

It's strewn with objects. Loose papers. A weapon crate.
A box of soft drinks, the cans spilled across the floor.

JOEL walks to the PIANO.

Plays a couple of notes.

Then turns to LEE.

Almost accusing.

                    JOEL
          This place is empty.

AT THAT MOMENT -

- a SQUAD of WESTERN FORCES SOLDIERS enter, from the
direction the journalists just came.

The JOURNALISTS and the SOLDIERS face each other for a beat.

Then the SOLDIER jabs a finger at them.

                    SOLDIER
          Stay the fuck out of our way.

They push past the journalists.

Moments later, there is a sudden burst of gunfire from
somewhere in the building.

It's muffled, but unambiguous.

It's almost immediately followed by a second burst. Slightly
louder.

LEE, JOEL, and JESSIE exchange a glance.

LEE'S gut was right.

The PRESIDENT is still here.

They set off, tracking the WESTERN FORCES SQUAD.

INT. THE WHITE HOUSE/PRESS OFFICE - NIGHT

The journalists approach an antechamber office, just off the
PRESS BRIEFING ROOM.

Ahead, the SERGEANT JO SQUAD have moved to the open door to
the PRESS BRIEFING ROOM.

A female voice is calling out to them.

                    FEMALE VOICE (O.S.)
               I am unarmed. I am alone. I am
               standing in the middle of the Press
               Briefing Room.

SERGEANT JO gestures to SOLDIER 1.

SOLDIER 1 takes a quick glance around the door frame.

Pulls back.

                    SOLDIER 1
               No weapon.

The WOMAN calls from the PRESS BRIEFING ROOM.

                    FEMALE VOICE (O.S.)
               I am Secret Service Agent Joy
               Butler. I am here to talk.

SERGEANT JO talks to SOLDIER 1.

104.

                    SERGEANT JO
          No weapon?

                    SOLDIER 1
          Looks like.

Beat.

Then SERGEANT JO lifts her rifle, then swings around the
door.

Steps into the room.

The other two SOLDIERS follow.

LEE moves forward to the doorway.

INT. THE WHITE HOUSE/PRESS BRIEFING ROOM - NIGHT

Through the doorway, LEE can see a long room. Almost empty.
Unused for some time. Arched windows. The curtain and
podium at the back of the room are still in place, and there
are a few chairs. Some tipped over.

At the far end, near the door to the West Wing offices, agent
JOY BUTLER stands.

Her hands are raised. Palms open.

The SOLDIERS have their rifles trained on her.

                    BUTLER
          I am here to negotiate the
          surrender of the President. Are
          you the WF?

                    SERGEANT JO
          Take a wild guess.

                    BUTLER
          Can the President be entrusted into
          your safe care?

SERGEANT JO has sweat rolling down her forehead. Running
into her eyes.

She doesn't wipe it. Blinks it away. Keeps her rifle
trained on BUTLER.

                    SERGEANT JO
          Yeah. Sure. Just bring him out.

105.

                    BUTLER
          We are not bringing him anywhere
          until we have agreed terms.

LEE lifts her camera.

Takes a shot.

                    BUTLER (CONT'D)
          We need a guarantee of safe passage
          for the President. And we need
          extraction to a neutral territory.
          We request Greenland or Alaska.

                    SERGEANT JO
          No terms. Bring him out.

Beat.

                    BUTLER
          Sir - the President is willing to -

She is cut off - as SERGEANT JO shoots her.

SILENCE THROUGH LEE'S LENS.

Agent BUTLER folds.

CUT TO -

- the three SOLDIERS immediately advancing to the far end of
the room.

As they move, another SECRET SERVICE AGENT appears in the
doorway to the WEST WING -

SILENCE THROUGH LEE'S LENS.

The AGENT is attempting to return fire.

He is immediately shot.

CUT TO -

- the SOLDIERS stacking by the door to the West Wing offices.

One lobs a grenade through the open door.

SILENCE THROUGH LEE'S LENS.

The detonation through the door.

The stacked SOLDIERS either side.

106.

CUT TO -

- the SOLDIERS pushing through the door.

Gunfire.

LEE moves forward.

JESSIE and JOEL follow.

INT. THE WHITE HOUSE/WEST WING/CORRIDOR - NIGHT

SILENCE THROUGH LEE'S LENS alternates with ACTION.

The ACTION is deafening. Totally kinetic. PURE INTENSITY.

The SILENCE is a Zen space. Only occupied by **IMAGE** and
SCORE.

The alternation is like a drumbeat. It has a kept rhythm.

ACTION

The SOLDIERS advancing down the WEST WING MAIN CORRIDOR.

SILENCE

A SECRET SERVICE AGENT is shot as he exits the CABINET ROOM.

ACTION

The SECRET SERVICE AGENT opens fire from the door to the OVAL
OFFICE, at the far end of the corridor.

SILENCE

The SERGEANT takes cover in the doorway to the PRESS
SECRETARY'S OFFICE.

ACTION

SOLDIER 1 gives return fire to the OVAL OFFICE, as SOLDIER 2
moves into the CABINET ROOM.

SILENCE

SOLDIER 1 fumbles as he reloads his rifle.

ACTION

The SERGEANT pulls a FLASHBANG from a vest pouch, and throws
it blind from the doorway, towards the OVAL OFFICE.

107.

SILENCE

The flashbang lights up the WEST WING MAIN CORRIDOR in stark white and etches out a SECRET SERVICE AGENT, emerging from the ROOSEVELT ROOM.

As he stumbles sideways from the shock of the detonation, he is cut down by bullets.

ACTION

LEE runs forward from cover to cover - a side corridor opposite the CABINET ROOM.

As she reaches the cover, rounds fired from the OVAL OFFICE slam into the wall behind her.

SILENCE

JESSIE and JOEL crouching behind the corner that leads back to the PRESS BRIEFING ROOM.

JESSIE is starting to move forwards to follow LEE.

JOEL is trying to catch her arm.

ACTION

JESSIE runs out into the WEST WING CORRIDOR -

- but in her adrenalin state, half panic, half courage -

- runs *past* LEE'S position.

AT THIS MOMENT -

The ALTERNATION between SILENCE and ACTION stops.

CUT TO -

SLOW MOTION

NOISELESS. But NOT THROUGH A LENS.

LEE seeing JESSIE.

The young woman framed in the corridor.

Turning back towards LEE - as if realising her mistake.

LEE'S hand - on her camera.

JESSIE turning - to LEE.

108.

Looking at her. Dazed. Confused.

Then -

- LEE'S hand releases the camera.

CUT OUT OF SILENCE AND SLOW MOTION -

- LEE pushing out of the cover of the doorway.

Throwing herself at JESSIE.

Knocking JESSIE to the ground.

CUT TO -

- the AGENT returning fire from the OVAL OFFICE.

- SOLDIER 1 falling backwards as he is hit.

- SERGEANT JO returning fire towards the OVAL OFFICE.

And right between the intense exchanges of fire -

- the two women.

CUT TO -

SLOW MOTION.

LEE.

In the REPLY IMAGE to the one she saw of JESSIE.

Standing, with the OVAL OFFICE behind her.

CUT TO -

JESSIE face - seeing this.

JESSIE'S hand tightening on her camera.

The camera LIFTING.

CUT TO -

SILENCE THROUGH A LENS.

But not LEE'S lens.

JESSIE'S.

On LEE. Framed perfectly.

As one of the rounds punches through LEE.

It exits her chest.

LEE lifts her head.

Looks straight down the lens of JESSIE'S camera.

Hold on this a beat.

Then -

- as the CAMERA SHUTTER fires.

CUT TO -

INT. THE WHITE HOUSE/WEST WING/CORRIDOR - NIGHT

- the corridor.

The shooting has stopped.

SOLDIER 1 lies dead.

LEE lies dead.

JESSIE sits on the floor. Her camera in her hands.

Staring at LEE.

The camera that lies beside her. Right by her hand.

JOEL walks down the corridor towards them.

As he reaches JESSIE, he stops.

Looks down.

After a beat, she looks up.

She looks like she did when we first saw her.

Just - young.

A beat between the two.

                    JOEL
              (gentle)
          Get up.

Beat.

                    JOEL (CONT'D)
          Get up, Jessie.

He reaches a hand out to her.

She takes it.

Rises.

INT. THE WHITE HOUSE/OVAL OFFICE - NIGHT

JOEL and JESSIE appear in the doorway to the OVAL OFFICE.

The desk.

The curved walls.

The south-facing windows.

There's a dead AGENT at his feet, and another dead agent in the middle of the room.

And on the other side of the room, the SERGEANT and SOLDIER 2 are dragging THE PRESIDENT out from behind the desk, where he has been crouched.

Without speaking - they drag him out by his legs.

Then SERGEANT JO reaches down.

Flips the man over, so he's face-up.

The PRESIDENT says nothing. Just looks confused. Hyperventilates.

Then SERGEANT JO rises, and pulls out her sidearm.

Points the gun down at the PRESIDENT.

                    JOEL
          Wait.

SERGEANT JO looks round at JOEL.

JOEL'S face is blank.

SERGEANT JO stares at him. But doesn't pull the trigger.

JOEL walks to them.

Stands over THE PRESIDENT. Finally face to face with the man.

Then JOEL lifts his digital recorder.

Beat.

> JOEL (CONT'D)
> I need a quote.

Beat.

> THE PRESIDENT
> ... Don't let them kill me.

JOEL nods.

> JOEL
> Yeah. That'll do.

SILENCE THROUGH JESSIE'S LENS.

As JOEL turns away –

– SERGEANT JO's gun arm straightens.

SERGEANT JO shoots.

Then, a beat later, she turns to look at JESSIE'S camera.

CUT TO BLACK.

END